Pride Publishing books by Peter E. Fenton

Single Books
The Woodcarver's Model

I0658953

THE WOODCARVER'S MODEL

PETER E. FENTON

The Woodcarver's Model
ISBN # 978-1-83943-788-5
©Copyright Peter E. Fenton 2022
Cover Art by Kelly Martin ©Copyright April 2022
Interior text design by Claire Siemaszkiewicz
Pride Publishing

Published in 2022 by Pride Publishing, United Kingdom.

THE
WOODCARVER'S
MODEL

Dedication

For Scott, who is my world.

Chapter One

He closed the door behind him and leaned against it as if his weight would hold out the world. How many of them had there been? When was he going to learn to think before he acted? This time he could have died. His heart raced. Fucking idiot! Where the fuck had Yussuf gone?

Rob woke with a start. From the look on the face of the passenger in seat 2B, Rob must have gasped or yelled. He was breathing heavily. Rob pressed the call button for the flight attendant. There was time for one more gin and tonic before they landed.

Once in the airport, after passing through customs, he retrieved his luggage from the baggage carousel. One large green canvas duffle bag – which looked more like it had been dragged by the plane rather than stored in its cargo hold – was all he had, other than his beaten-up leather shoulder bag. He made it out to the cab stand and took the next available taxi.

"Queen's Quay Terminal building, please," he said to the driver, then closed his eyes. He didn't want to appear to be rude by not talking. *So Canadian*, he thought. The *oh-look-I've-fallen-asleep* ruse usually fended off any attempt at mindless chatter from a driver. And he didn't need to see the sights. The ride from Toronto's Pearson International Airport to his home on the lake shore was nothing to see. It was all highway, industrial complexes, stubby office buildings and shopping malls. The trip showed Toronto as the ugly, unimaginative metropolis that it was, until they hit the expressway by the lake. Then it all changed — the lake, so big that it looked like a sea, the gaudy glamour of the Palais Royale dance hall, and the century-old buildings of the Canadian National Exhibition — they still made Rob smile. A quick left onto Queen's Quay and he was almost home.

During the cab ride, he thought of his last night in Mogadishu. Of returning to his hotel room after dinner with his photographer. The Hotel Mustaqbal on the traffic-jammed Wadada Uganda was one of the better accommodations in this war-torn country. Clean rooms with a fair certainty of hot and cold running water. What else could he have asked for in Somalia?

When he'd entered the room, he had sensed, without even turning on the lights, that everything had been tossed. He'd frozen, not wanting to make a sound in case the intruders were still there. Whoever'd done this was probably looking for his computer, jewellery, identity papers — anything of value. The joke was on them. He'd learned years ago never to travel with electronics, other than his phone, and he kept that and his identification on him at all times. And he wrote everything in notebooks. He never had to worry about notebooks. No one wanted them, they didn't break and they didn't run out of power in a jungle. He'd once lost his pen in Tierra del Fuego but was still able to finish writing using a charred stick from the fire.

As he had surveyed the damage in his hotel room, he'd heard a noise. Out of the corner of his eye, he'd seen a figure make for the window. It was Abdi, his driver. Abdi had thrown himself out the window onto the fire escape. Rob had chased him. Why? He didn't know.

They'd both hit the main street running. Rob had run right past a man leaning against a car talking to someone in front of the hotel. He'd kept going for another few hundred yards before realising it had been his guide, Yussuf. It was a few blocks later, on a small side street, that Abdi had yelled something in Somali to a few men. One had pulled out a gun and started firing at Rob. Rob had been pinned in a doorway, shards of concrete flying all around him, when he'd heard more shouting. More firing. *Where the fuck was Yussuf?* Then there was silence. Finally, a familiar head had poked around the corner.

"It's safe now, boss. You come. Come!" Yussuf had waved him to follow. In his hand, he'd held an old CAR-15 automatic rifle. A body lay in the street. Rob hadn't stopped to see who it was.

Life as an adventure travel writer was not what he thought it would be when he began this job. There was adventure, and there was this. One of these days, the adventure was going to win and all of the Yussufs in the world would not be able to save him.

* * * *

"Just by the water taxi stand, please."

The driver pulled over to the curb. Rob paid the fare, wished him a good day, then toted his bag over to the pier.

The water taxi was a small open boat that ferried passengers from the mainland to one of the Toronto Islands. Formed from sediment washed from the Scarborough Bluffs to the east, the islands had once been a large sandbar which extended as an unbroken spit into the waters of Lake Ontario. Hurricanes in the mid-1800s had severed what were now the islands from the mainland. Over the years, houses, some no more than holiday shacks, had cropped up. Larger homes had followed. SeaBreeze, a modest three-bedroom, two-storey house with a roof deck, had been built in the late 1960s by Rob's parents. They'd seen it as a needed quick-access get-away from their busy urban life. It was now the place Rob called home.

The sign for SeaBreeze, pegged to the front door, had been hand-carved by a local craftsman who'd missed the space after the *Sea*. Rob's parents had found it charming and wouldn't let him re-carve it. Here, Rob was at peace. It was just him, the trees and Lake Ontario. The sounds of waves on the shore and the cries of the birds were the only music he needed. They reminded him of his parents, and they were good memories.

He walked through the front door and everything was as he'd left it. All except for the dishes in the sink and the black bra on the floor under the baby grand piano. He was fine with that. At least, he would be fine with it as soon as he tidied everything up. And as soon as he'd settled in, he would call his cleaner to book an appointment.

As much as Rob thrived on chaos in the field, home had to be...organised. It was his problem, he realised that, but this was his home. Karen, who took care of the place when he was on assignment, was, to put it politely, a slob. *"Look after your house? Of course I don't mind. Why would I? You've seen where I live. Looking after a flophouse would be a step up in the world."* It was because of Karen that he'd bought the piano. He couldn't play a note. It had to be tuned regularly because of the lakefront humidity, but that didn't matter because Karen loved it, and she could play like Billy Joel.

Anyone seeing this house and hearing that the owner was a travel writer might think that writing was quite a profitable venture. SeaBreeze, with its luxurious finishes and lake view, could lead them to that conclusion, but they'd be wrong. Rob Hanson made little money. Some years not enough to cover expenses. This lifestyle was thanks to his parents — structural engineers who'd specialised in large-scale hydroelectric projects. They'd flown down to inspect one of their constructions on the Marañón River in Peru when their plane had gone down. That was twenty years ago.

Rob felt that he'd had a happy childhood. His parents had been his best friends. They'd treated him like an adult from an early age, openly discussing their lives, sharing their fascinations and friends with him. He had always felt safe, comfortable and loved.

He'd been raised by his parents in an old Victorian house on South Drive, in Toronto's Rosedale neighbourhood, one of the city's wealthiest communities. It was the home of the old-time gentry — of merchants, doctors and lawyers, of inheritors of money that no longer seemed to work for a living. The other two most affluent neighbourhoods, Forest Hill and the Bridle Path, were built for a different sort, each with its own...requirements. Rosedale, for instance, was the realm of the old white Anglo-Saxon Protestants. Rumour had it that even during the latter part of the last century, people couldn't purchase there if they were Jewish. The wealthy and well-connected Jews and foreign émigrés established themselves in Forest Hill, an enclave of newer stately homes constructed a little further from the centre of their world — Toronto. The third neighbourhood, the Bridle Path, was for the gaudy nouveau riche — entertainers and entrepreneurial magnates — who desired large mansions and larger properties still within the confines of the metropolis.

Homes on South Drive, like their owners, were on the modest side of wealth. Rob's parents had been accepted there despite their lack of historic connections, by virtue of being *clever people*. A neighbourhood like Rosedale liked clever people. It wore them like a Hermès scarf. Clever people made the other people feel chic and intelligent.

What Rob loved most about South Drive was its proximity to the Moore Park Ravine, a large expanse of wilderness in the city. He'd spent most of his free time there, exploring, making trails even deeper into his own private jungle. Here, his imagination had run wild. Here, he had learned the names of every tree, shrub, animal and fungus. Here, he had taught himself how to photograph everything from the largest tree to the smallest insect. But, more importantly, he'd learned to love, respect and understand nature.

Rob had been in his mid-twenties when he'd heard the news that his parents had gone missing. Their plane had gone down in the Peruvian jungle. When he'd received the news from an old family friend, a company lawyer, there'd been a bit of a disconnect. He'd heard the words, but his mind had only focused on Peru. *That's where Paddington Bear came from. Deepest, darkest Peru. I wonder if they'll meet any bears?* Why a twenty-five-year-old would have that thought had never occurred to him at the time.

He had been flown down to the area by his parents' company during the search. Karen, whom he'd known since university days, had come along for support. Rob's sister, Jessica, thought too young to be involved, had been left in the care of their aunt.

It had taken authorities three weeks to discover the tangled wreckage of his parents' DHC-7. Rob had held Karen's hand as they were flown to the crash site by helicopter. There'd been no sign of human remains left at the site. He and Karen hadn't spoken. They'd clasped hands and focused on breathing. Neither had experienced death up until then.

As he'd stood in the jungle, surrounded by shards of debris, Rob had cried. He'd thought of never seeing his parents again, not knowing if they got out of the plane in time and were still out there…lost. Or had the animals… No, he wouldn't let his mind wander there. But the more he had looked around, the more he'd felt, as inappropriate as it might have seemed, that in some strange way, his parents would have liked this as their final resting place. They'd both loved the wilderness. Rob had stayed on-site for the following week as the search continued, and the longer he stayed, the more peace he'd found. It was there that he had discovered what he wanted to do with his life — explore the wilderness.

When his parents' estate had been settled, including the sale of their company, Rob Hanson discovered that he would never have to fear for his financial future. He'd become one of Toronto's most eligible bachelors.

Chapter Two

Rob stood in his living room and noticed something. Or more appropriately, smelled something. It smelled of rot. *Dammit! She's forgotten to throw out the garbage again. How many times do I have to remind her...* Then he realised it wasn't the garbage—it was him. A gunfight followed by a night of drinking and a forty-hour commute with two layovers could do horrible things to a man's aroma. Rob Hanson needed a shower more than anything else in the world.

As Rob towelled dry, he looked at himself in the mirror. *Not bad.* Most guys his age had a bit of a gut. He didn't. At one hundred and sixty pounds, he had a slim waist and a rock-hard stomach, although it wasn't exactly a six-pack. Living on a diet of hotel and field food didn't make that possible, but the physical demands of the job kept him in damned good shape...for a forty-five-year-old who was five-foot-eight inches tall. He still had a great head of hair, dark brown verging on black. His eyebrows were full and accented his grey-green eyes. A firm, square jaw and perfect white teeth — *thank you, Mom and Dad, for the orthodontics* — lent to a model's good looks.

His shoulders, arms and thighs were thickly muscled as a result of a heavy gym regimen. A strong body had saved him on many occasions in the field. Rock and mountain climbing required strong limbs in order to survive. And, speaking of physique, he had to admit his *lower appendage* was something else to admire.

He wandered down to the kitchen, towel wrapped around his waist, and grabbed a beer from the fridge. As a thank-you for letting her stay there, Karen always made sure the fridge and cupboards were well stocked with his favourite foods when he returned. Of course, he'd given Karen a credit card to cover those purchases. Musicians didn't make enough money to buy the kind of food he liked.

He wandered back up to the rooftop deck and leaned against the railing, taking in the view. No matter how much he loved to travel, coming home was the reward for the inevitable pains.

His neighbour, an artist by the name of Gwen — just Gwen — was out in her front yard sunning topless. She liked to do that. It annoyed the tourists who forever streamed by on the pathway that cut in front of their properties *"like a slash across the gut of a murder victim"* — Gwen's words, not Rob's.

"Hey Gwen," he called down, raising his bottle to her.

"Hey Rob. Just get back?"

"Yup."

"Come on over in a couple of hours if you want. The Kirbys'll be here for drinks."

"I'll keep that in mind. Thanks." He wouldn't. He hated the Kirbys. So did Gwen, but they brought pretentiously expensive wine wherever they went.

The phone rang. Rob knew he should get it. It would be Karen. She knew he would be back by now. He answered.

"Hello."

"That's all I get—hello?"

"Hello, most beautiful Karen, protector of hearth and home." As he spoke, he bowed and his towel slipped to the balcony floor. He caught it before a large family group, who were passing by, caught sight of him.

"Closer," she said, hinting at the desire for a better compliment.

"That's all I got. Oh—are you missing a bra?"

"You found it? Where the hell did it get to?"

"I didn't think bras had a habit of getting to anywhere by themselves."

"You'd be surprised."

"Well, this one got under the piano."

"That sneaky little bastard. Oh, I remember now. There was this huge fly, you see. It was so big, I mean biblical-plague big, and it was buzzing around driving me nuts so I thought, 'What do you use to kill something biblically big?' A sling. You know, like Davey slew Goliath with."

"I think you mean David and Goliath. *Davey and Goliath* was a Christian-centred cartoon from the… Oh, never mind." He stopped before giving the full history of the cartoon he'd grown up with. Karen hated when he interrupted her with one of his academic diatribes.

"Like I said—biblical. So, I took off my bra, loaded an apple into the cup, swung it around and let her go."

"Did you get the fly?"

"No. It's probably still there. But the apple went through the open window and I assumed my bra did as well."

Rob had hoped it had been the result of some wild sexual fling. Karen didn't socialise enough.

She continued, "I'm so glad you found it. It's one of my favourites. You have no idea how hard it is to find the perfect bra."

"You're right there. I have no idea. Hey — thanks for the" — he looked at the beer label — "Wheel Rat. It's not bad."

"It's what they were serving at the symphony season opener last night and I thought it tasted pretty fine."

"Did you steal it?" he asked suspiciously.

"Of course not. I liberated it and twenty-three of its friends from the grimy hands of the oppressive ruling class."

He smiled. "Who knew the oppressive ruling class drank Wheel Rat?"

"Yeah, I know, right? So, I hope the trip went without a hitch."

He stopped smiling. "As hitchless as a trip can go." *Why worry her with the details?*

"So…any hot guys there for you?"

Here it comes. The lecture. She did this every time.

"Well, there was Abdi, but I think he was just interested in my money."

He heard her sigh on the other end of the line. "Is it too much to ask that you find someone and settle down? How long has it been?"

"We're not going down that road. Not now."

"I just want you to be happy."

"I am happy," he said. *In my own little screwed-up way.*

She wasn't giving up. "You know what your problem is, don't you? You're terrified of commitment."

"That's not true."

"You avoid any chance of it."

"How do you figure that?" he shot back a little too quickly.

"Well, for starters, your only close friend's a girl, and we both know I don't have a chance, but you don't have any guy friends at all... I mean, to increase your odds of a successful relationship, you have to start somewhere."

"Don't be silly. I have plenty of guy friends."

"Name one."

He struggled for a moment before coming up with, "Carl at the gym."

"The towel guy? Do you even know his last name, or maybe where he lives, or whether he's a dog or a cat person?"

"Last names among gay men are not necessarily... necessary."

"Do you have *any* guys you're close to?"

"Why would I need to? I have you."

She shot back, "I think you're using me as a shield so you don't leave yourself open to meeting a guy you could fall in love with."

"Wha... That's crazy talk."

Rob wasn't ready for this conversation. Why did everyone assume that he needed a relationship? He didn't need anyone to get in the way. And as for any physical needs... Well, if he couldn't handle them himself, he could easily find someone who could. Like Carl from the gym. Whatever his last name was.

"Sorry, hun. I've got a call coming in that I have to take," he lied. "Dinner later this week?"

"Of course. Love ya."

"Love you too."

"Now, if only you could learn to say that to a guy."

"Gotta go."

He disconnected from the call. Rob took a deep breath, then took a long draw on his bottle of Wheel Rat and stared out into the harbour. *I'm fine with things just the way they are.*

Chapter Three

After a good long sleep and a light breakfast, Rob sat at his desk, coffee within reach, typing away at the keyboard, transcribing his notes, occasionally writing out phrases and making structural comments which would form the shape of his story. And what a story this one would be. A sixty-thousand-word tale of ugliness and violence among a beautiful people who could not be crushed. *This* was what he lived for — shining a light into the dark, illuminating a path into a new world for his readers. Now, if only he'd been shot on that last night. Not seriously, just a flesh wound. He would have had Errol photograph it. A nice rich black-and-white image focused on the wound. What a cover that would have made for *One Man in Mogadishu*. It would be a bestseller. He needed one of those right about now. It had been five years since *One Man Against the Mountain* had won him the Governor General's Award for non-fiction and a modest film deal. It wasn't a huge amount of money, but how many people could claim that Tom Cruise had played them in a film?

His phone rang. Rob was so focused on his writing he answered without checking caller ID.

"Rob Hanson."

"Robert, sweetheart. How are you?" said a raspy voice that spoke of years of too many cigarettes and too much scotch. It was Estelle, Rob's seventy-year-old literary agent.

"Estelle. How are you?"

He stood and took his coffee into the living room. A call from Estelle could last a while. Through the window, his eye caught the sight of a majestic three-masted tall ship sailing towards the harbour.

"…invoice from Errol." There was a long pause on the phone. "Are you even listening to me?" she asked.

"Sorry, Estelle. The brain's still a bit drifty. What did you say?"

"I asked if it was all right to go ahead and pay the invoice from Errol?"

"Of course you can. Wait—you never ask me about things like that. What's up?"

"How was your trip?"

There was another long pause as he looked out the window. He'd always wanted to take a cruise on a ship like that. It took him back to his childhood —

"Look, if you're too busy right now…"

"No. No…ah. It was great. I think the manuscript will write itself. In the meantime, I can come up with a teaser piece for you to send out to the magazines."

"That's what I like to hear. So, it all went smoothly," she coughed out.

"Couldn't have gone smoother."

"Aside from the street killing."

Rob hadn't planned on telling her this soon. "Who snitched?"

"You keep secrets from me, Robert. I keep some from you. Look, I'm not your mother. I don't judge you. You don't judge me. So, now that the gunfight at the OK Corral is over and done with, I need you to do me a favour. You like islands?"

"Y — es," he said hesitantly.

"I figured. You live on one, after all. Anyway, my friend at *West Coast Travel* magazine needs a quick two thousand words on Marsh Island. Ever heard of it?"

"Never."

"Neither have I. But Cedric needs an article and I'm not about to let him down."

"Cedric," Rob thought aloud. "Isn't that the name of the guy you've been seeing?"

"Yes, Mr Nosy. He flies into Toronto for *visits*, and he's the best lay I've had since the first Trudeau was in power, so I'm not about to fuck this up. So, are you going to help me out?"

"If it'll help your sex life, you bet." He laughed.

"Good. Now, his secretary's sick so you'll have to sign the contract when you get out there. Okay?"

"Sure thing."

"And thanks for not making me beg for it. I get enough of that from Cedric. Now this'll be a nice, gentle piece after Somalia."

"So, where is this place?"

"Who the hell knows and who cares, other than you, of course. It's probably one of those little rocks off the coast of Vancouver. I thought it might be a perfect excuse to visit Jessica."

"Jessica?"

After a moment she threw him a lifeline. "Your sister."

"Crap."

"I thought you might like to visit her… Her birthday's coming up." She coaxed him into putting the pieces together.

"Crap again."

"It'll be her thirty-fifth, so you can stop taxing that poor brain of yours. Strangely, it falls on the same date as it did last year. And *you're welcome* for remembering."

Chapter Four

The flight from Toronto to Vancouver took the prescribed five hours. Rob liked to spoil himself on planes. Business class — never first. That would be overkill. Even in business class, the comfortable seats, better food and drink, and cuter flight attendants made it almost worth the extra money it cost, and he could write it off as a business expense.

Colin — that was the flight attendant's name — brought him almost everything he wanted. Rob wasn't about to make a total ass of himself by pretending that the attention the cute young man was paying him was anything other than a professional courtesy. Older men would fall for that. Rob wasn't about to become one of them. In the time it took the plane to fly across the country, Rob was able to have a fine meal, several strong drinks — which he would need to fortify himself for the day he would spend with his sister — and, most importantly, the chance to just stare out the window at the world below. The vastness of this country never ceased to amaze him. He could fly to Iceland in almost the same time it took to travel to British Columbia. It took twenty-four hours of nonstop driving just to cross the province of Ontario. Was it any wonder that with a country so large, people in this nation had trouble understanding each other?

He stared out the window as the plane flew over rock-rimmed lakes, past prairie expanses to mountain foothills, then from foothills over the Rockies, all while his fellow passengers around him watched the same old movies for a second time while the greatest show on earth was just outside their windows. *Idiots*, he thought.

Once they had landed and the baggage handlers had somehow magically got his flight's luggage from the plane to the right carousel, he found his one bag — Rob always travelled light when he was working — and made his way to the cab stand where he grabbed a Yellow Cab. Why did every large city have a company called Yellow Cab?

"Sylvia Hotel, please," he said, and the cab took off with little more than a "Yes, sir," from the driver. If the cabbie didn't kill him on the way, or take him far off the acceptable route, this guy was going to get a very good tip.

The Sylvia was Rob's favourite hotel in Vancouver. It was old, reasonably small and comfortable. He even liked the name. Something like he would expect of an elderly aunt or aged female friend. It sounded reliable and discreet.

The cab pulled up beside the hotel on English Bay in twenty minutes. A big tip it was. Inside Rob was greeted at registration by a smiling, older woman who remembered him from an earlier trip when he'd had a holdover on his way to Hawaii where he'd been covering the booming volcano tourist trade.

"Good evening, Mr Hanson. So nice to see you again." She had obviously checked the list and records of registering clients at the start of her shift. This was why he liked the Sylvia.

"I have you down for one night."

"Just a quick stopover. A birthday party." He hoped that hadn't come across as too arrogant. A little arrogance was fine. Too much was trashy.

"We have the English Bay Suite for you, if that's okay?"

"Perfect," he replied, as he smiled and nodded. No chit-chat. She processed him quickly and warmly. He'd been here before and didn't need to be told anything about the restaurant, the seawall walk or the hotel cat, Mr Got To Go.

He was in the suite for no more than ten minutes when his cell phone rang. Without even looking at the caller ID, he answered.

"Jessica. Perfect timing," he lied. He always lied to her. It had become a habit. Jessica had ruled over his life since their parents had died. She'd been fifteen at the time and was convinced that their mother and father had been involved in uncovering an environmental wrong-doing and had faked their deaths to pursue the evildoers. She'd expected them to rise from the dead and return to her as heroes. Rob had been in no position to take care of a young woman, especially one with such a vivid imagination, so she'd been farmed out to their mother's sister, Coco. They had called her Cuckoo behind her back. Her real name was Gertrude.

Even at fifteen, Jessica had bossed Rob around like he was the younger sibling in spite of the fact he was ten years older, and things had never changed. Jessica, who Coco had always called Kitty — *did anyone in that generation believe in using one's given name?* — had moved to Vancouver as soon as she'd come of age and had control over her inheritance. Now, one might assume hers would be a story of squandered wealth — young girl moves to cosmopolitan city and fritters away her money on shoes, martinis and good-looking young men. No — that was not Jessica. She had turned out to be a master of finance, trusting no one and doubling her net worth in ten years. She even handled Rob's investments. Rob wasn't foolish enough to ignore her advice.

"I expect you to be here at seven sharp," she said.

"I'll be there. Are you still drinking red?"

"The darker and thicker the better." With anyone else he might have made a joke out of her comment, but he knew Jessica better than that.

* * * *

Jessica Hanson lived in a condo at Alberni and Jervis in Vancouver's West End. It was only on the second floor, but that allowed for a nine-hundred-square-foot terrace which put his roof deck to shame.

It was a designer's dream. Paintings covered every wall and they, like everything else in her suite, were modern and exquisite. It was less than a half-hour's walk from his hotel to her place. He stopped along the way to pick up a bottle of wine and a simple teardrop pearl on a platinum chain for a birthday present. He might not have liked her at times, but he sure as hell loved and appreciated her.

The concierge let him into the lobby and, after introductions and a check of the guest list, buzzed him into the inner sanctum. Rather than take the elevator up one floor, he jogged up the marble staircase to her door, one of two on the floor.

He rang. The door opened and Jessica stood there smiling, a glass of wine in hand.

"Robby," she cried out. She threw her one arm around him, taking care not to spill any wine. "It's been two years since you've been out here."

"There's nothing stopping you from coming out to see me, you know." He tried to keep the sarcasm to a minimum.

"Yeah, right. Now get yourself in here and tell me what you've been up to." She spirited his bottle away, placing it on the dining room table, and handed him a glass of what she was having. "We'd better finish this off before we crack open your bottle."

Jessica led him out onto the terrace where a table was laid with enough hors d'oeuvres to feed an army. He took it all in—a large sectional, multiple chairs, tastefully arranged, lush greenery, sculptures and a water feature—no, it was a pond. With koi.

They clinked glasses. "Happy birthday. Oh, by the way, I got you something. I didn't have time to wrap it."

He handed her the present.

Jessica opened it. "Thank you, it's beautiful." She put it on, smiled and gave him another hug. "So, tell me what you've been doing."

"Well, I just got back from a trip," Rob replied.

"No surprise there. Where this time? Mountains? Deserts?"

"Somalia."

"Who the hell travels to Somalia on vacation?"

"You'd be surprised," he said, without adding, *Well, me, for one.*

The doorbell rang.

"I'll be right back." She smiled. He looked around again. He could have a koi pond on his roof deck if he wanted it. *Except the gulls would eat them all in a day,* he thought. Moments later he heard a male voice. Soon Jessica and a *gentleman caller* joined Rob. He was an older man, probably in his mid-fifties. Some would say distinguished, meaning nicely dressed — though a bit too formal — but well-groomed with a good head of hair.

"Robert," Jessica began.

Why did she call him Robert? She never called him that unless...

"I'd like you to meet Thomas Koss. Thomas, this is my brother, Robert." The gentleman caller approached and held out his hand.

Rob noticed his perfect teeth and signs of a slight paunch under his jacket. Rob shook his hand and smiled back. *Jessica, I'm going to kill you,* he thought.

"Nice to meet you. Jessica's told me so much about you," Thomas said.

"I bet she has."

"Let me get you a glass of wine," Jessica said before leaving them alone.

"I hear you are a writer. Adventure travel, is it?"

"Yeah," Rob replied, before swallowing down the remaining wine in his glass.

"How did you get interested in that field?"

"It started when our parents were killed in a plane crash in the jungles of Peru."

"Oh God, I'm so sorry. I didn't know," Thomas said, with a horrified look on his face. Rob smirked inside at the reaction, desired as it was. But he decided not to play the guy...at least not too much.

"Not something my sister would have brought up in business conversation. I assume that's where you two know each other from."

Thomas looked relieved at the change of topic. "Yes, we work at the same firm."

Jessica returned with a wine for Thomas. "White for you, isn't it?"

"Thanks." The gentleman caller took a healthy sip of the drink.

Jessica noticed Rob's glass. "That went fast," she commented, with a bit of an edge.

"Thirsty, I guess." Rob smiled, handing it back to her. His raised eyebrows hinted at an unspoken *Please, I'm going to need more.* "Hot walk over here. So, Thomas—" Rob started.

"Please. Call me Thom." Rob swore he could hear the *h* in the way he pronounced his name.

"Thom... So, you're with Jessica at Bloombury, Peake and Squire? The investment arm as well?"

"No. I never had any real talent at money. I'm in legal."

Jessica returned with Rob's glass refilled and a full wine bottle, which she plunked down on the table nearest him.

"A lawyer," Rob said, throwing a smile at Jessica, who looked mildly confused. He turned back to Thom. "Were you always interested in law?"

"It runs in the family. Both my mother and father were lawyers."

"Were they? That's nice, children following in the footsteps of their parents."

"And what do your parents do?" It was clear from the look on Thom's face that the sentence had slipped out before his brain had been able to stop it.

Not a good trait in a lawyer, Rob thought. *Probably practices contract law.*

"Oh God, I'm so sorry!" Thom exclaimed.

The entire evening went that way. Throughout dinner, Rob enjoyed baiting Tom-with-an-H, although it took so little effort. It was like fighting off a puppy. After Thom had left, claiming an early morning meeting, Jessica turned to Rob the moment the door was closed.

"What the hell was that about?"

"Having fun? I wanted to see how many times he could put his foot in his mouth before the evening was done."

"You can be such a bastard." Jessica stomped back to the terrace and Rob followed.

She poured another glass of wine and sat down on the sectional. "So, no hope at all?" she asked.

Rob sat down beside her. "Next time maybe you can try to set me up with someone I might find more of a challenge. I hope he's better at handling himself in court."

"He's a contract lawyer," she said, sounding embarrassed.

"I knew it!" Rob laughed.

Jessica glowered. "Well, I'm glad you had fun. Can you even imagine what work will be like next week? I'll have to wear a bag over my head."

"I suspect he'll be the one wearing the bag. His type's more likely to be handing in his resignation."

"I told him you were such a nice guy. Smart. Well-travelled. I told him you helped build an orphanage in Syria, for Christ's sake."

"Well, what did you expect when you try to set me up with someone? And what the hell did you think I'd have in common with him? You heard him. He probably ties bows in his dog's fur."

"He seemed so stable and…"

Rob saw her trying to hold back tears. "I'm sorry," he said. "I was nasty tonight."

"Yes, you were."

"It's just that…when I want to have a relationship, I'll find someone. On my own terms."

She looked at him with concern and said, "But it's been such a long time since you and Kevin split. Was it so bad that it put you off men entirely?"

"Oh, trust me. I still like men."

She took his hand in hers. "It's just that you seemed so happy back then. I miss that."

"I'm still happy," he assured her.

"Oh, come on. When was the last time you laughed?"

"Other than tonight?"

"You are such a jerk," she said, swatting him with a throw pillow.

"And that's why you love me. Look, that thing between Kevin and I ended up… It was horrible. As sucky as it sounds, it hurt like hell. I honestly wanted to die, and it took years before I stopped feeling like a hollow shell. The last thing I need, or want, is another person in my life making a mess of it. I like it just the way it is."

She hugged him. "I'm sorry."

"It's okay. You were just trying to help."

"I meant I was sorry about what happened between you and Kevin. I'm not apologising for tonight."

"No, I wouldn't expect you to." He laughed.

"So...you don't see anything happening between you and Thom?"

"No."

"Not even a tiny spark?" she asked hopefully.

"Not even static."

"I'm going to have so much explaining to do come Monday," she said, burying her face in her hands.

Rob smiled a lot on his walk back to the hotel. Tom-with-an-H was an unmitigated disaster, but Jessica loved him enough to try, and that was what mattered. *Oh God*, Rob thought. *When did I become so sentimental?* He wondered if it was age, loneliness or a combination of both, but Rob knew that sentimentality made him uncomfortable. He pushed the thought away and focused on getting back to the hotel. Perhaps it was the wine, but something inside of him was sounding a small alarm bell. *Something's coming. Don't let your emotions get out of control.*

Chapter Five

Rob had initially thought he'd fly from Vancouver to Victoria but opted to rent a car and take the ferry instead. It gave him more flexibility in scheduling, and he loved to be in control of things.

He had researched Marsh Island online before leaving Toronto and found almost nothing about it. *The island is like an undiscovered world. You can barely find it on a map. No wonder they wanted an article on it.* He was uneasy going into a situation knowing so little about it, but it was still in Canada, so how bad could it get? Just the same, he thought he'd better rent something with traction and a winch. And while he was at it, maybe get a pontoon boat.

He arrived at the local car rental office, a short walk from the Sylvia, at nine in the morning. They had his Jeep Wrangler cleaned, fuelled and ready for him when he got there. Sadly, they had no pontoon boats. After a brief walk-around inspection, he tossed his duffle bag in the back, adjusted the seat and mirrors and headed out on the adventure. At least with this one, no one should be shooting at him — he hoped.

Rob had two choices — drive north to Horseshoe Bay and take the ferry there, or head south and take the ferry from Tsawwassen. The ferry trip from Horseshoe Bay was less picturesque than the southern route, but it was shorter, so it won. He'd get in quickly, talk to the locals and get out as fast as he could. A strategic strike was what he was looking for. He could make anything sound desirable to tourists.

The drive to the Horseshoe Bay ferry terminal from Vancouver's West End took him through Stanley Park, still looking a bit sad after the windstorm of 2006 which had blown down ten thousand trees, including countless giant redwoods. An old-growth forest wasn't something that could be replaced in fifteen years. That being said, Rob felt at peace driving through the four-hundred-and-five hectares of lush vegetation.

From Stanley Park, it was a twenty-minute trip along the winding coastal highway to the ferry terminal where Rob joined the boarding line.

The air smelled of the sea — salt, fish and algae. It hit his sense memory like a halibut to the face. With each deep breath, the tension in his body released and a calmness crept over him. An announcement signalled all passengers should return to their vehicles as boarding was about to commence.

Once his Jeep was parked in the car bay, he made his way to the passenger deck where he started taking some shots around the ship. His process was to take as many images as he could. Pictures formed the article. Formed and informed. He loved photography — stealing moments of time, capturing emotions. It was photographing the jungle in Peru as they searched for his parents that had allowed him to hold on to his life as he knew it—to hold on to his sanity. It was later in life that he saw the benefit of taking a photographer along with him. Besides being a second pair of eyes to capture those split-second events that eluded him because he was looking in the opposite direction, they could also capture Rob. He became, in some pieces, the story.

A young man sat by the window of one of the observation windows. The sun shadowed his face to perfection, his cheekbones, perfect nose and the slightest smile showing his pure delight in the sight of the island they were passing. Rob rapidly fired off a number of shots. The young man was pure beauty in that instant, never to be repeated. He had captured his soul. Rob sighed and took in a deep breath.

Up on the deck, he shot off a few more frames. In his mind he still thought in terms of frames and rolls of film as if he still used them. There was something more tactile, more romantic, in the old photographic form. He caught himself—*There you go, being sentimental again.*

"Excuse me. Your camera…it's a Phase One IQ5, isn't it?" The voice came out of nowhere and Rob jumped, almost dropping the camera.

"Oh shit, I'm sorry," the voice from behind continued. "I didn't mean to scare you."

Rob turned around and it was him—from the observation cabin—and he was even more beautiful out here with the wind blowing his hair than he was when Rob had first noticed him.

"Oh, no problem," Rob stuttered. "I just didn't hear you. I was focused on those circling hawks and…"

"Ha—focused... Photography joke. Good one," the young man quipped.

My God, he's younger than I thought. Maybe twenty? An angelic twenty...

"So is that the Phase One IQ5?" The guy was persistent if nothing else.

"Yeah, it's the IQ."

The boy's eyes glinted like they were taking in a pile of gold, which was about what the camera cost. "It's the unicorn of cameras. You hear about them but never see them."

Rob replied, "They're perfect for wilderness work. Small, lightweight—"

"*And they can take the shock of a falling rock,*" the guy said, and laughed. A sweet, pure sound. Like a church bell, if the church was a gorgeous, five-foot-ten, white-blond-haired twenty-year-old.

"Oh—from the ads. Right." Rob smiled. "Well, it's true. I was caught in a minor rockslide on the side of a mountain with a camera like this a number of years ago, and it still worked. Better than I did," he said, indicating the scar running down his left bicep which he shamelessly flexed. The boy's eyes lingered a little too long on it, Rob noticed.

"So, you're a pro?"

"Somewhat. More of a writer, but sometimes it's best to take your own pictures. Your eye and your writer's brain are on the same wavelength so it's easier to match images to the words you're going to write. They don't fight each other or have to compromise." *Hey—that was pretty good,* Rob thought. "Do you want to try it?" Rob handed the camera to him.

"Shit, I never thought I'd get to see one of these let alone...they're so freakin' expensive."

"It's always best not to think of that when you shoot. Go ahead. Give it a try." Rob pointed out into the world, giving him permission to use the camera.

"Can I?"

"Fire away. And if there are any that I can use, I'll pay you for them and give you credit."

"Really? Fucking amazing!"

The boy took to the camera like a pro. "We have nothing like this in school."

"And where's that?"

"Emily Carr," he said, focusing his attention more on the camera than on Rob. Rob focused his attention on the boy. For the first time in a long time, he felt that flutter in his chest. It wasn't as much the looks of the guy, or the youthfulness; there was an intensity, a passion that radiated off him. It was palpable. Rob just wanted to reach out and — *Grow up. Don't touch.*

"You'd better take this back or I'll just end up filling your memory card. This thing is amazing. It's so…intuitive. It becomes part of your hand and eye."

Rob smiled. "I'm not kidding. If there's something in here that works with my story, I'll pay you for it and give you credit. Here, let me get a shot of you." The boy posed against the railing just as the wind caught his blond hair and tossed it perfectly across his face. "I might even use that one. Now I'll audio-record you. Just state your name, email address, then I'll ask you another question about usage rights and if you're okay with it, say that you agree."

"This is wild." The kid laughed. He introduced himself — Kyle Marshall, with two l's — and gave his email address and his permission to use any images he had taken. "For credit and payment," he added.

Now it was his turn. Rob took out a business card, which made him feel old enough to be his father, and passed it to Kyle. The young man glanced at it and his jaw dropped.

"You're Rob Hanson? *The* Rob Hanson? *One Man Against the Mountain?*"

"Yeah." Rob let out a modest giggle before catching himself. "The same."

"I just got my picture taken by Rob Hanson, holy shit. I ate, slept and dreamt that book when it came out. That was one of the reasons I wanted to get into wilderness photography in the first place. Wait here. Please don't move. My boyfriend's gotta meet you. He's gonna flip out."

Boyfriend. Of course he has a boyfriend. Why would anybody that perfect not have a boyfriend?

A few moments later Kyle returned dragging a buff twenty-something porn star/gymnast with him. Rob wasn't sure which would be his next move — throwing himself or the porn star off the ship.

* * * *

When the ship docked, Rob got into his Jeep and headed off. He had plenty of time to catch the 3:50 ferry departing from Nanaimo to Gabriola Island. Then it was a short ten-minute private ferry ride to Marsh Island.

On the ferry from Nanaimo, Rob asked around to see if anyone knew anything about Marsh Island. He found one talkative passenger who didn't know much about the island itself, but did know a bit about the married couple that ran the ferry, in spite of the powerful BC Ferries Services' regional monopoly. She explained the rumour was that the only way the McKinnons had managed to hold on to the Marsh Island licence was due to the self-serving influence of their local Member of the Legislative Assembly, Hugh McCutcheon. Frances and Francis McKinnon's opinions were respected by the islanders and a word from them could win or lose him a good number of votes.

Rob pulled up to the Marsh Island ferry dock in good time for the next crossing. A large, not-so-pleasant woman sauntered up to the driver's window. Her nametag identified her as Frances. She put her foot on the running board and leaned her two-hundred-and-ten-pound bulk towards Rob. The Jeep heeled noticeably to one side.

"Ye-ah?" she said.

"One passage to Marsh Island," Rob replied.

"You not coming back?" she countered. Her jaw kept moving after the question which confused Rob until he realised she had a plug of chewing tobacco tucked in her cheek.

"Well, yeah. In a few days if all goes well."

"You comin' back, you gotta pay for a return trip."

"Oh. Okay. One return ticket, please. How much will that be?"

She pondered this complex question a moment.

"Well...return for a car's fifty dollars. That's Canadian dollars."

"Fifty Canadian it is," he said in as friendly a manner as he could muster and started to reach for his wallet.

"You goin' with it?"

"Well...that's kinda the way it works, isn't it?"

"Usually, but I ain't no mind reader." She just stood there staring at him. Rob wasn't sure if she was putting him on, or if her problem ran deeper.

"How much for a car and driver, then?" he offered back.

"You don't live there, do you?"

"No." What he wanted to say was, *If I lived there, would I have to ask these stupid questions?*

"Car *with* driver…non-resident driver'd be" — she did the math in her head — "sixty bucks."

"Sixty bucks it is. Do you take credit?"

"Prefer cash."

"But you *do* take credit if I don't have the cash, right?"

She chewed her plug of tobacco and pondered. "No. Not set up for cards."

"Okay, cash it is." Rob reached into his wallet and pulled out three twenties and handed them to her. She took the bills and carefully counted them out.

"Git on." She pointed to the small, flat-decked scow called the *Frances 2* that lay in front of him. He wondered if renting the pontoon boat would have been a safer choice.

When the small ferry fired up its engines, Rob fired up his courage and approached Frances, who was standing at the bow.

"Since I've invested so much in this voyage, I was wondering if you would answer a question?" he asked.

"Depends."

"On what?"

"The question," she snapped back.

Rob paused, then plunged onward. "Who would I talk to about what it's like to live on the island?"

"Marsh Island?"

"The very one."

"Fair question." She looked him over as she pondered his query for quite a while, then said, "Well, most folks ain't gonna give you the time o' day. It ain't that they're not friendly. It's just they're suspicious of strangers. I'd look up the woodcarver. He knows the island and likes to talk. You can find him at tomorrow's market. He's got a booth there."

"And where would I find the market?

"That's two questions. Your fare only gets you one."

* * * *

What Rob knew about Marsh Island could be easily summarised. It was the northern-most island in the archipelago at the south end of the Strait of Georgia. It was a little more than fifteen square miles in size, rising to almost eight hundred and fifty feet high at the summit of Mount Admiral. Its population was three hundred and seventy-three at the time of the last census. The economic engine of the island now lay in the garden market business—a reasonable amount of that being, until recently, the under-reported pot-growing industry—as well as craftsmen, writers and painters. The islanders were an extremely self-sufficient and private society who preferred to limit the influence of the outside world—except for tourists willing to leave their dollars in Marsh Islanders' pockets.

Rob eased the Jeep down the ramp onto the tiny Marsh Island pier. First things first—he'd check into the island's only hotel, The Marsh Inn. Their mascot was a little green fellow with antennae. *How quaint.* He should have enough time to scout out the island before dinner. Tomorrow he'd find the marketplace and the recommended woodcarver and make an appointment to interview him if he thought he'd be of any use.

There was no signage to show him the way into town. His Jeep's GPS maps had nothing on this place, so he turned right. After driving for ten minutes, he noticed his mood lifting. The road, really no more than a lane and a half wide, was bordered by tall trees which formed a green canopy over his head. He opened the sunroof. The air smelled fresh and salty. The sunlight trickled through the overhead leaves. He stopped the Jeep and stepped out onto the road. He filled his lungs with air and he began to smile.

Rob reached back into the Jeep, pulled the camera out of his pack and, for five minutes, photographed the light-dappled road — a British country lane transported halfway 'round the world.

Rob was so into his own moment and place in time, that he failed to sense the car coming up behind him being driven at high speed. The driver also failed to see him, or notice that his Jeep was not in motion, and had to slam on the brakes in order to avoid hitting the oblivious tourist. The air was filled with the sound of rubber sliding on gravel and a horn blaring. Rob's utopic moment was over.

"What the hell are you doing?" yelled a tall, middle-aged woman as she leapt out of her car. "Are you *trying* to get yourself killed?"

"I'm so sorry. I…" Rob excitedly pointed down the road. "This. Is. Heaven!" He got this way at times. A beautiful moment in nature brought out a child-like state of euphoria in him. He became a five-year-old at Christmas. That was what made him the eco-travel journalist he was.

"Come here. Let me show you." He took her by the arm and placed her in front of the Jeep and proceeded to show her the images he had just captured on his camera. Some showed the contrast of brilliant green leaves against the pale blue sky above, while others revealed beams of light streaming through the foliage, spotting the multi-tonal shades of brown and grey of the road like a painter with a brush.

"My mother called them God's eyelashes," he told her.

She smiled, then said, "Well, you've certainly got an eye for nature, but you can't just stop in the middle of the road. You could get yourself killed."

Still scrolling through his pictures, he said, "It would almost be worth it to have seen something like this."

"You aren't from these parts, are you?"

"No, but I can see why people would want to be. I'm Rob, by the way. Rob Hanson," he said, extending his hand.

She shook his hand and replied, "Sheila Marsh. So, what brings you to the island?"

"I'm an explorer, I guess. I go places I've never been — never dreamt of wanting to go — and I let people know that there's a whole great big beautiful world out there waiting just for them." He was beaming as he spoke.

"Well, Mr Rob Hanson, you go on exploring. Just don't get yourself killed while doing it — even if you think those pictures are worth it."

"I promise. Am I going the right way to get to the Marsh Inn?"

"The way you're going, you'll wind up in the cemetery."

"I told you," he said, smiling, "I promise to be more careful."

"I appreciate that, but the direction you're facing will take you to the cemetery…and my vet clinic. The Marsh Inn is back that way. Now if you don't mind, I've got a ferret that needs attending to."

Sheila got back into her car and edged around Rob's Jeep.

He stared after her and was going to say something, but the light caught the haze of the dust from Sheila's car as she drove away, and instead he instinctively reached for his camera and snapped a few more shots. The people here weren't the friendliest he'd ever met, but the island had a certain charm and for the first time in a long time, Rob started to feel relaxed. As he got back into his Jeep, the voice in his head said, *This is where you're meant to be.* And for some reason, he knew that it was true.

Chapter Six

The man ran his hands across Mitch's chest.

"You've been working out."

Mitch was too stoned to speak.

"You like that, don't you? Your nipples are hard. I didn't know you were such a pig."

Mitch had trouble focusing. The world was black and white and grey, like a low-budget film from the sixties.

His mouth was filled with cotton wool, his legs, with lead. He saw his arms moving like they were floating in water. His hands were conducting a slow orchestral movement.

The man rubbed his shoulders.

"God, you are so tense. I know what would make you feel better. It'll calm you right down."

He knew the man's voice, but the face… There was no face. Just a grey sack. And a sharp stab in his arm.

Mitch woke with a start, gasping, soaked with sweat.

* * * *

Mitchell Carcross made a living, of sorts, selling the bowls that he carved out of salvaged wood from the forests of Marsh Island. On occasion he carved trays, stools and even the odd table and chairs, but those were special orders. The bowls were an easier sell, since they were small enough to be toted away by a tourist, and easier to justify. *"Look. It'll hold things!"*

Tomorrow he would sell his wares at the Saturday market in town, but today he had two prospective buyers in his workshop—a future bride and groom from Nanaimo looking for gifts for their bridal party.

"You should try to get on one of those studio tours. You could make a killing selling these things."

He didn't want to tell them that it would be a pretty short tour, his being the only studio on the island, *studio* being a rather pretentious word to describe the oversized shed they were standing in.

The young couple stood in front of a large table covered in wooden bowls. Different woods, different styles, some with live edges revealing the natural exterior of the tree and some so thin that they looked as if they would break just sitting there.

"Those look fragile, but they can hold up to use," Mitch said, picking one up and rapping it a few times on the table.

"Impressive," the man said, lifting a bowl and gently tapping it. "Well?" he said to the woman, "what do you think?"

"I don't know. I think Becky and Caitlin would like the fancy ones," she said, indicating the one that had just gone through the torture-test, "but I think Karla would like the rough-and-tumble one."

"The guys'll just want one that'll hold a bag o' nuts, and one they wouldn't have to worry about breaking when they knocked it off the table."

"I'd recommend a selection of styles. That way the recipients will know you chose the bowls specifically for them. I find there's nothing worse than giving a bunch of people the exact same gift. For the guys, I'd suggest bowls from the natural line," Mitch pitched in, referring to the bowl that looked rough-hewn from a tree burl. Personally, Mitch hated those. There was no finesse in producing one. "For the ladies, something more refined…except for Karla. She seems to be more the practical type."

"That's one way to put it."

"Don't go there, Dave. I've warned you. If she prefers girls to boys, that's none of your business."

"I'm not saying anything!" he replied, then to Mitch adding, "She could wrestle a trucker into the mud and out-cuss a sailor."

"Don't you go talking about my sister that way."

Mitch guessed that this relationship had less than a fifty-fifty chance of survival.

In spite of that, he made the sale of six bowls for five hundred dollars.

"But when I saw your bowls at the market the other week, they were fifty dollars each."

"Oh, those were carved for the tourist trade. These ones are the real thing made from a better grade of wood, slow-aged for stability," Mitch lied. Soon after meeting them, he'd decided to levy an Asshole Premium on any sale he made.

He wrapped the bowls in plastic bubble wrap, boxed them individually and, with wishes for a happy marriage, bid the couple a fond farewell.

Once the money was deposited in the Bank of Cookie-Jar, Mitch poured himself a congratulatory glass of wine, sat on the porch of his house and stared out into the peace that surrounded him. The sun was just beginning to set as a shooting star made its appearance in the eastern sky.

Chapter Seven

The Marsh Inn and Restaurant was on the main road from just beyond the cut-off Rob had taken to the cemetery. It was hard to miss with its six-foot-high green Martian cut-out — which looked suspiciously like the Great Gazoo from the *Flintstones* cartoon — complete with a cartoon bubble declaring, "Don't be a dum-dum. Our food is yum-yum."

"How bad could it be?" Rob said to himself.

The inn itself was an impressive, large two-storey clapboard house complete with a widow's walk. More than likely, it had originally been the home of a wealthy seagoing man. It was painted a soothing sage green with accents of yellow and rust on the ornate gingerbread trim and pillars of the covered porch which encircled the house. Much to his delight, there were Adirondack chairs scattered all around. Rob loved nothing more than sitting on a porch and watching the sun go down. He opened the wood-framed screen door and stepped into the lobby.

Carol Gough was the proprietor of the Marsh Inn. She greeted Rob with a warm, unpretentious smile. "You must be Mr Hanson."

"That's me," he answered. He liked her already.

"Well, welcome to the Marsh Inn. Now, I have you down for three nights."

"Would it be possible to extend that if I'm kept here longer?"

"No problem at all. Right now, it's only you and a nice young couple from Nanaimo."

After taking care of registration, he noticed the time — seven-thirty. He glanced towards the door of what he thought was the dining room.

Carol smiled. "The restaurant's open if you're hungry."

"I'm starving, actually. I don't think I've eaten more than a sandwich all day."

"Well, you go and drop your bags off in your room. Freshen up and come on down. What are you drinking? I can have it ready for you."

He thought for a moment. "What do you have in the way of reds?"

"Amarone, shiraz or merlot? The amarone is heaven."

"Heaven it is. I'll be right back."

Rob went up to his room on the second floor and discovered it had a view over the water. It was like he was back at SeaBreeze. He was going to enjoy his stay here.

He entered the dining room and was greeted by his server, Marla. She was Carol's daughter. "I've seated you nearer the fire, but not too close. We want you comfortable, not sweltering."

His glass of wine was waiting for him. He sipped his way through it while his dinner was being prepared. He decided to let the chef choose. It was a seafood lover's delight—salmon, scallops and oysters formed the base, with a light salad on the side and a glass of sauvignon blanc.

A young couple joined him in the dining room. He watched them interact and caught snippets of conversation. They were obviously getting married and there seemed to be some friction regarding her sister. He ordered them a bottle of champagne on his tab.

From encounters with a beautiful young photographer to a sun-dappled country lane and now this meal, the day had been perfect. He took his wine out onto the porch. It was nearing sunset and a shooting star arced across the eastern sky.

* * * *

Rob awoke refreshed after a good night's rest. He had a light breakfast in the dining room before heading off in his Jeep for a drive around the island. The market wouldn't be open yet, so he had some time to explore.

He got himself turned around leaving the inn and ended up back on the country lane. He passed the veterinary clinic, which had several trucks parked in front, and soon found himself at the cemetery.

It was an unpretentious country graveyard. He started to photograph it. There was the formal entrance—two stone pillars with a wrought iron arch bearing the name of the 'Marsh Island Burying Ground.' It wasn't fenced in, just open to the woods on one side and the sea on the other. The headstones were plain—some simple stone plaques. Even the largest monument, one to Josiah Marsh, carried no ornamentation, only a name and dates. *They must be Protestants.*

"Lost again?"

Rob turned to find Sheila Marsh standing there, a bouquet of wildflowers in her hand.

He smiled. "Just touring the island. Business, this time."

She smiled back. "You in the cemetery business?"

"Only if the cemetery's interesting enough to write about."

"Ah. A writer."

"Guilty as charged," he confessed.

"So — are we interesting enough for you?"

"I've taken dozens of shots so far. It's a beautiful spot. Peaceful."

"Like a cemetery should be," she agreed.

Rob watched as Sheila walked by him and placed the flowers at Josiah's grave. She kissed her hand and touched the stone with it. "It was his birthday yesterday. I don't think he'll mind if I'm a day late." She turned to leave. "Have a nice day," she said without looking back.

"Thanks. You too. Tell me, what time does the market open?"

"Ten. It's usually busy at first with people looking for deals."

"I'd better get moving then," he said, and they walked out of the cemetery together.

* * * *

He found the market in a small field across from an adorable century-old Anglican church. He parked the

Jeep on the road, but rather than trying to find the woodcarver right away, he spent a few minutes photographing the church, inside and out. *This will make the perfect intro shot for the article. Who wouldn't fall in love with a fifty-seat chapel?*

He wandered about the small marketplace taking random shots as he went — a young couple selling food preserves, an apple-doll-faced woman with her handmade quilts, a middle-aged fellow selling his knit and felted clothing — all pretty standard fare for this kind of event. But at the end of the row stood one booth which captured his attention. A cluster of people — probably a tourist family, Rob imagined, from the range of sizes and ages and their clothing — were all vying for the attention of the handsome young man behind the counter. This was the woodcarver.

Rob took a few photos from a distance. He checked one, zooming in on the booth to check composition and focus, and noticed the eyes of the woodcarver looking directly at him. It both startled and excited him.

As he neared the booth, he overheard the carver say, "No, the bowl's carved from a burl. That's a swelling on a tree trunk." That was followed by, "I don't know if Burl Ives was named after a swelling on a tree. It would make me worry about his parents if he was," at which point the woodcarver looked away from his clients and focused on Rob. Rob swore he could feel the man's dark eyes — physically feel them on his face. The man redirected his gaze, and a wide smile showed off his beautiful white teeth. White teeth against tanned skin, complemented by lustrous long dark hair and the scruff of a beard — Rob had to remember to breathe.

He continued to watch from a distance and decided not to approach the woodcarver until after his sale was completed…and he was sure it would be completed. No one would be able to resist that man's magnetism. Rob wandered over to an adjoining booth where the proprietor was selling crocheted… Rob wasn't even sure what they were, when he heard, "Sally — do you mind me borrowing your visitor for a moment?"

"No problem at all, Mitch. He doesn't look like a corgi-cosy kinda guy," she answered.

Corgi cosy? Rob thought.

"You look more like the kinda guy who'd be interested in hard wood than polyester yarn." There was that smile again, and the eyes that locked onto his.

Rob laughed nervously. *What the hell are you doing?* he thought to himself.

"Sally knits little coats for dogs. She calls them Corgi Cosies. You just pop them on your dog like you would a tea cosy over a pot of tea."

"That's what she meant? I never would have guessed."

"It takes a bit of time to understand an islander. It took me years."

"So, you're not from here?" Rob asked.

"No," the carver said, smiling. Damn, his teeth were perfect. "I came from out east. From Ontario."

"Me too," Rob squeaked. *Stop sounding like a hormonal ten-year-old.* "Look, I was told that you were the one to talk to" — he stammered — "if I had any questions about the Island."

"Aw. Are people talking about me? Used to be they'd only say things to each other behind my back. Now they're telling perfect" — as he said the word, he touched Rob's shoulder — "strangers." Rob was ready to buy whatever he was selling.

"Uh—the name's Rob," he said, offering his hand to this flawless specimen of masculinity whose eyes still bored straight through his own and deep into his soul.

"Mitch." He smiled back, taking Rob's hand in his. If Rob's heart had fluttered at that young man's attention on the ferry, it just about stopped with this one.

"So, what do you want to know?" he continued, finally releasing Rob's hand.

"I'm here to write an article on Marsh Island for a magazine."

"Cool."

"You were recommended by the ferry operator."

"Frances? God, does anything escape her?"

"What do you mean?"

"Oh, private joke."

"Do you mind if I get a few shots of you and your carvings while the light is still good?"

"Oh. Sure. Fire away."

Rob worked with the camera. This guy was a perfect model. He could have been a professional. His facial expression varied from joyous smiles to steamy intensity.

"So, how long have you been living here?" Rob asked, taking another angle.

"About ten years now," Mitch answered, slightly adjusting his pose.

"Did you carve before coming here?"

"It's what I studied in school—Emily Carr in Vancouver."

What do they put in the water at that school? Rob thought. *I've gotta write a story about that place.*

"But there my medium was marble, not wood," Mitch continued.

"So, I guess you know all of the sights on the island? The ones that would interest a visitor?"

That beautiful smile intensified. "I know pretty well every nook and cranny *intimately.*"

Is this guy flirting? With me? Please let this guy be flirting with me…

"There's not an inch of this island I haven't explored," Mitch said.

"Well, it looks like I've found my man — if you're willing and available, that is."

"Ready, willing and able," he said. "But I don't come cheap."

"Of…of course not," Rob stuttered, for some reason with embarrassment.

"Dinner'll be on you."

"My pleasure."

Rob was just wrapping up shooting as dark rain clouds began to form and the shoppers gave up watching from the sidelines. If he never took another picture in his life, he would still have these.

It was then that Mitch asked, "You don't remember me, do you?"

Confused, Rob said, "What?"

"You don't remember where we know each other from."

"Oh, trust me, I'd remember you."

Mitch grinned. "Is that so, Hanson? Rob Hanson, right?"

"Yeah — I introduced myself when we met."

Mitch smiled, and pressed on. "Just your first name. No Hanson mentioned. And definitely nothing of *Handsome Hanson.*"

"Handsome…" Then it came to Rob. "Mitch! Mitch Carcross?"

"One and the same."

Rob chuckled. "Kevin's little brother."

"That's me. But I've grown up a bit since we last saw each other."

"You sure have," Rob said, with a little too much enthusiasm.

Mitch grabbed him up in a great big hug.

Mitch had been a scrawny, pimple-faced boy of thirteen when Rob and Kevin had split. *Split* was not quite it, was it? It was not a word used to describe the fiery eruption that had ended that romance, the one true joy he had felt in his adult life...a part of his life from which no evidence remained. Until now.

Mitch hugged him and Rob hoped it would never end.

"Come on. Help me pack up before the rain comes."

* * * *

They had just finished up the grilled salmon and vegetables Mitch had prepared, in spite of the deal that dinner would be on Rob. They moved into the living room. Rob brought the bottle of wine.

Rob nestled into the overstuffed sofa and watched as Mitch threw another log on the fire. *So little Mitchell Carcross has a house*, he thought, *and not just any house — a beautiful, cozy, post-and-beam, one-storey, half-way-up-the-mountain-at-the-edge-of-the-woods-overlooking-the-Strait-of-Georgia house.* Could this really be the annoying little kid who had kept pestering him twenty years ago?

"This place is beautiful," Rob said, looking around.

"I love it here. It is absolute tranquillity. It's the only house on Mount Admiral."

"How did you swing that? I'd have expected the mountain to be prime real estate."

"It would be if the islanders let it. Which they won't." Mitch sat down in the chair opposite Rob. "They're nice people, but they don't take to strangers, and they don't like things to change. Many years ago, a crew came to the island to look at putting up a cell tower, and they were held hostage here by my Aunt Sarah until the company changed its mind. This house..." he said, looking around with love, "this house was hers, so don't go getting any ideas that I'm rich. She lived on the island for most her life. Everybody loved Sarah. I used to come over from Vancouver to help her out when she got sick. I did build the wheelchair ramp outside, so some of the work on the place is mine." He smiled. "She left it to me in her will and that's how I was able to move here to the island." He shifted ever so slightly on the couch like he wanted to change the topic. "Are you okay for wine?" Mitch asked.

Rob smiled. "I seem to be empty."

"Must be the high evaporation rate," said Mitch as he refilled both of their glasses. "The islanders are good people. Not to say we don't have our fair share of colourful characters."

"Like who?"

"Off the record?"

"You bet."

"Farley Dougald dresses up in women's clothing."

"Lots of guys do that."

"But it's why he does it that's interesting. It's quite a touching story, actually. He and his wife ran a small dairy farm. When she passed away a few years back, the cows dried up. Farley figured they missed his wife as much as he did. He wondered if they'd find comfort in a female presence, so he dressed up in one of her old work dresses and gave it a shot. His cows have increased their milk output since he donned that dirndl. Then there's Maggie Tupman who, at eighty-six, greets every sunrise standing at attention on the eastern bluff in the buff while singing the national anthem. Colourful enough for you?" Mitch took a swig of wine. "They may at first seem a bit stand-offish, but they really are warm people."

"Frances didn't seem to be the motherly, welcoming type."

"Well, she and her husband, Francis, are our first line of defence with that little ferry of theirs." Mitch sat down on the couch beside Rob, twisting himself to face him, his foot pressing against Rob's knee. "The people here just want to protect the island. They've seen the ownership on the other islands shift from the full-time residents to part-timers from the mainland, a lot of them from out-of-country, and they don't want that to happen here on Marsh. There's a fear that with mainland taxpayers comes a loss of the traditional way of life."

"Sounds a bit protectionist, doesn't it?"

"Of course it does. They're fighting for their way of life, and it's not a bad one. People around here watch out for each other. They help each other. That workshop you saw coming in here, that was built with the help of my neighbours. A regular old-time barn-raising that was, and without them I wouldn't have a business. They don't try to keep people out based on race, religion or even sexuality. God, why do you think Frances told you to come and see me? She tries to set me up with every good-looking single guy who comes across on her ferry."

"Okay, that answers one of my questions," Rob said, as his heart rate increased.

"Yeah, my parents were so proud. Two for two, and one of them an artist to boot."

"Speaking of the other one, do you see Kevin at all?" Rob asked cautiously.

"Oh, yeah. He spent some time with me in the spring. He was drying out, he said."

"That's good to hear."

"So good that he says it every time he comes for a visit."

"Oh."

"If you don't mind me asking, what happened between you two?" Mitch asked.

Rob was silent for a moment.

"You don't have to talk about it if you don't want to," Mitch said, sounding vulnerable for the first time.

"No. You should know." Rob took a sip from his glass. "Kevin's drinking had been getting a bit out of hand, but we were what, twenty-five? We'd gone out to a restaurant—just a small local mixed place, we drank way too much and he caught me kissing some cute waiter in the bathroom. It was nothing more than that—a drunken kiss. Your brother went ballistic. It carried on out into the restaurant where a straight co-worker of Kevin's was having a few drinks with friends. That guy ended up spreading the news at work that the hot office jock was a faggot. In those days, being gay wasn't as accepted in the world of sports journalism as it apparently is here on Fantasy Island. Anyway, Kevin was fired."

"I knew he'd been fired, but he never said why."

"And it gets worse. When he was told he was canned, Kevin punched the boss in the face. That led to a short spell in jail —"

"Wait," Mitch interrupted. "He told me that was for unpaid speeding tickets."

"Yeah, well…after that, he couldn't get another job in his field. That led to even more drinking and who knows what else. He blamed me for everything."

"I had no idea. I'm sorry. I just knew you guys split." Mitch blushed. "I fantasised that you broke up with him because you were secretly in love with me."

"You were thirteen!"

"I know, but I knew what I was and what I wanted. And that just so happened to be Handsome Hanson."

Mitch shifted his position on the couch and leaned over. Rob stopped breathing. Mitch closed his eyes as their lips met. His body continued its forward momentum and he lay on top of Rob. Their lips parted. Mitch's tongue slid past Rob's teeth, penetrating his mouth and soul in one strong motion. Rob wrapped his arms around Mitch's torso. He felt every muscle, well defined by hard work. He slid his right hand up Mitch's spine, running his fingers through the thick black hair as he pressed the woodcarver's mouth harder against his. Rob inched his left hand down Mitch's back, stopping on the mounds of his perfect ass, which Mitch flexed in teasing pleasure, pressing his crotch into Rob's.

Mitch pulled away just long enough to say, "I think you've had too much to drink to drive home."

"Yeah. Too much."

"I think you'd better spend the night."

"Yeah. Smart."

"Just to play it safe."

"Yeah. Safe.".

Chapter Eight

Rob woke up with the morning sun in his face. He was alone. Well, not entirely alone. Two great big brown eyes stared up at him from the end of the bed.

"Well, hello."

He hadn't seen the dog last night. Maybe Mitch had kept him locked up so he didn't get in the way.

The dog stood up, turned and started to leave the room. Then he paused and looked back at Rob to make sure he was following.

"Okay. I'm coming."

The dog left the room and Rob stood and stretched. He felt well rested. He rarely, if ever, spent a night at someone's place. It was usually a quick kiss after the deed was done, a few spoken pleasantries and false promises and a quick exit. He slipped his underwear and jeans on as he took in the spectacular sea view out the window, then he followed in the dog's footsteps.

The moment Rob left the bedroom, he heard the sound of feet stepping and sliding, and a mixture of humming with an attempt at a few sung words. There was Mitch, in front of the kitchen counter, wearing nothing but boxer briefs and his headphones, dancing and singing softly to a song as he made breakfast. In a partial spin, he saw Rob.

"Good morning! I see you met Rufus. I sent him in to get you up. If I'm going to show you the island, we'd better get an early start."

How is it possible for someone to look this good in the morning? Rob thought.

"First, I'm going to put you to work," Mitch said. "Mugs are in the cupboard. I take milk in my coffee."

"You got it."

As Rob walked past him, Mitch gave him a kiss. And not just a quick thanks-for-the-fuck kiss, but the kind that could lead to never getting to breakfast.

"Later," Mitch said, flashing that brilliant smile at him.

Rob poured Mitch a coffee and handed it to him. "I didn't know you had a dog."

"Oh, I don't, really. Rufus doesn't belong to me. He's kinda his own dog, if you know what I mean. He just sorta shows up now and then to check up on me, don'tcha boy?" Mitch scratched the dog's head and Rufus made a strange, pleasant yowly talking sound. "He's a one-dog neighbourhood watch."

Their island tour began at the kitchen table and Mitch was as excited as a child at Christmas.

"First we have fresh fruit from the Williams' place down the road. Try this." Mitch picked up a blood-red strawberry, dipped it in yogurt and rubbed it on Rob's lips until he opened his mouth, licking the yogurt off the berry before slowly biting into it.

"The yogurt was from Maggie. You remember — the naked sun worshipper? The venison sausages are from

Matty Tsugami. He hunts his own meat. Okay — that's from the mainland, but he grinds and stuffs his own," he said.

"I just bet he does," Rob replied, smirking.

"Very funny. Now, the eggs, they come from Sheila Marsh out by the cemetery and before you say anything, yes, they come from her chickens, not her personally. Finally, the granola…I made that myself," he said with pride.

"This is great. It's all so great. You should consider opening your own restaurant," Rob said, for which he received a kiss from the chef. "You mentioned Sheila Marsh. We ran into each other yesterday. She seems nice and…normal."

"She's the island veterinarian. A great person."

"So, are her family the Marshes of Marsh Island?"

"She's the great-great-great-granddaughter of the first European to settle here, or something like that. The Marshes were sailors and fishermen, mainly. Josiah Marsh settled here first, which is why the town here is called Josiah. Before him, the island was inhabited by the Coast Salish. Sheila's the best to talk to about that. I know you can still see their petroglyphs in the rocks along the shore where Mount Admiral dips into the sea."

"Amazing."

Mitch grinned. "We'll see some of them on our trip if we ever get out of here. Mind if Rufus joins us? He likes car rides."

Rob looked at Rufus. "How could I say no to a face like that?"

Rufus yowled in approval.

* * * *

66

After breakfast, they headed out in Mitch's truck, a beat-up pickup with a crew cab. Just the sort of vehicle needed to haul wood and the occasional dog. They had to work out the seating arrangements as Rufus usually travelled in the front passenger seat and wasn't convinced that the newcomer should get preferential treatment. It was soon decided that Rob could sit in the front seat if Rufus could sit in his lap. At a shifting sixty pounds, Rufus was quite a load, but he soon learned the benefits of a human seat which would hold him in place on the bumpy journey.

The first stop was back in town where Rob paid for his one night of unused accommodation at the Marsh Inn and cancelled the rest of his stay. Carol Gough was quite pleased to hear that he had discovered his childhood friend living on the island and invited him to come back any time.

After picking up a couple of cups of decent coffee for the road, and a few bottles of water for Rufus, they headed on to pay a visit to some of the locals Mitch did business with. Bartering was an important way of life on the island. Some fresh-cut herbs for a dozen eggs, a wooden bowl for home preserves, aged beef for a rustic bench. Everyone looked out for everyone else. Rufus decided to stay at the butcher's for a while, so Mitch and Rob headed off on their own. Life for Rufus was like life on a sixties commune in the age of free love when switching partners was not seen as a personal slight, but an opportunity for adventure.

"Our next stop is a special one for me," Mitch said, as they headed off the island's coastal road and up a more rustic route. The truck climbed through the trees up a road that was more rutted track than legal passage.

I'm glad it's not my rental we're taking up here, Rob thought.

"Good thing Rufus isn't in your lap," hollered Mitch as he shifted gears and the truck bounced its way over rocks and around fallen branches. After twenty minutes they reached a barren polished rock outcrop and Mitch pulled over.

"Come on. We'll hoof it from here." They left the truck and as Mitch took Rob's hand, they re-entered the forest. Walking holding hands was a new thing for Rob. He and Kevin had never held hands when they walked. It felt...odd. He let go for a moment.

"Sorry, I..." Mitch started.

"No. It's not that. It feels... I think mine needs to be the other way."

Until then, he had never thought that there could be a right way to hold someone's hand. Like in other aspects of intimacy, there was a top and a bottom. Kinesthetics dictated that the hand of the taller member of the partnership took the more vertical, or *top* position in the holding. Being shorter, Rob shifted his hand to the horizontal one.

"There," Rob said. He was pleased with his discovery. "You see — now I'm the bottom." He smiled.

Mitch laughed out loud. "You are so delightfully weird." Then he grabbed Rob and kissed him deeply. They continued through the woods, hand in hand, top and bottom, as it should be.

After a few minutes, they stepped out of the trees into a clearing. The world opened up and blue sky replaced the green canopy. In front of them lay an ancient, cracked granite mound thirty feet high. They climbed. In a few minutes, they reached the summit.

"Welcome to Admiral's Peak, the highest point on the mountain," Mitch said as some might introduce a newcomer to the Sistine Chapel.

"Holy…" Rob said in awe.

"Exactly." After a long pause Mitch said, "I come here when my mind is cloudy and I need to find peace." He squeezed Rob's hand.

It wasn't, by far, the tallest peak Rob had ever climbed — Everest held that claim — but it was nevertheless spectacular. A three-hundred-sixty-degree vista of sea, forest and mountain. And the air — that salt-tanged, oxygen-filled, organic freshness that worked its way into the blood and brought peace to the soul. Places like this were rare on earth. To find one on this island…tears filled Rob's eyes. Mitch wiped a tear off Rob's cheek.

"This is right and good," he commented, holding up his dampened finger. "I wonder if the Coast Salish thought of this as a sacred place. I do. So did Aunt Sarah. We should be grateful to be here."

Mitch looked away into the distance. Rob could see his lips move ever so slightly in near-silent prayer. Maybe, if he was lucky, Mitch would teach him that prayer. Some day.

* * * *

As they wandered back down through the woods, they came upon a small stream of clear water. Mitch knelt down, cupped some up in his hands and brought it up to Rob's lips. Rob drank it in.

"This comes from a spring just up that hill," he said, indicating a small rise to their right. "This place provides you with everything you need to sustain yourself, body and soul."

They walked on and Mitch continued the lesson.

"Bullrush roots, of course, and the corms of the yellow glacier flower. Camas, which is a member of the asparagus family. Salmonberries are good, they look like orange raspberries," he explained, becoming more excited, "and soapberries contain something called saponins which allow them to be whipped up into something like ice cream."

Rob smiled at his enthusiasm. Mitch was showing off what he loved.

"Then there are a number of fungi, like oyster mushrooms and puffballs, that are edible, as well as grubs and insects that are high in protein.

"No thank you. I've eaten a lot of things from around the world, but insects...not for me."

"Don't knock it until you need it, mister," Mitch said with a smile.

"You seem to know a lot about edibles in the forest."

"They can save your life," Mitch responded. "They saved mine."

Rob sensed that he shouldn't push on that subject.

"We should probably get going," Mitch suggested.

They climbed back down in near silence. Rob held Mitch's hand even tighter as if it would prevent the moment from ending. When they reached the truck, Rob turned to face him. Their faces were inches apart.

"Thank you," he said, and they kissed.

As the truck bumped and rocked its way back down to the main road, Rob had found the strength to speak again.

"What I felt up there, on the Peak, I haven't felt like that in twenty years, not since I went looking for my parents when their plane crashed in Peru."

Mitch put his hand on Rob's thigh. "I'm so sorry."

Rob continued, "I went down to help with the search. I was probably far more trouble than I was worth, but they let me stay. I kept wandering off from the main search party, but I never got lost, and this was in a part of the world where expert bush men could lose their way in a single turn. I never felt scared, or alone. It was as if my folks were there with me the whole time, watching over me. I felt peace like I'd never felt before. Until now."

They drove on slowly for a few minutes, then Mitch broke the silence. "The first time I felt peace like that was when I was in the rainforest in Ucluelet on the west coast of Vancouver Island. I stood beside a seventeen-hundred-year-old tree. I remember thinking that when that tree died and toppled, it would still serve a purpose in the forest's life, nurturing seedlings for another fifteen hundred years. Imagine making a difference for thirty-two hundred years — even Christ can't claim that. It made me feel so insignificant. It made my problems feel even smaller."

The truck rounded a sharp turn and Mitch slammed on the brakes. "Would you look at that? It's perfect. Come on." He hopped out of the truck and Rob followed.

Right on the edge of the track lay a thick tree limb. One end was partially charred.

"Lightning strike," Mitch said. "Here, give me a hand."

They picked it up. It felt like it weighed over two hundred pounds. As they manhandled it back to the truck, Mitch's arm and shoulder muscles bulged under his tight shirt. *No wonder he's built that way,* Rob thought, wanting nothing more than to rip that shirt off his body and lick the sweat from his iron-hard limbs. They threw it in the back of the truck.

"There. I'll be able to make something out of that when it dries. Now, I'd better get you home so I can deal with that," he said, pointing to Rob's swollen crotch.

"Do we have to wait?"

"Probably not," Mitch said, dropping to his knees.

* * * *

They pulled up to Mitch's house. *I wonder if Rufus made it back okay?* Rob thought.

"One more thing to show you, then I think some food'll be in order." Mitch said.

"Thank God. I'm starving."

"First, let's grab that tree limb."

They wrestled it out of the back of the truck and Mitch said, "This way." About a hundred yards behind the house stood a small barn—more of a large shed, with a barn roof. This was Mitch's workshop, the one built with his neighbours. They propped the tree limb under a large roof-covered wood pile.

"Come on. Let me show you my toys."

"Kinky," Rob replied.

"Is your mind always in the gutter?" Mitch laughed.

"Around you, yes."

"Well, you'd better keep it in your pants because there are things in there that could easily take it off. Even one as big as yours." Mitch reached back and gave Rob's crotch a squeeze.

"Not fair!" Rob cried. "Now you'll be to blame for anything that happens in there."

The building was about fifteen by twenty-five feet in size, holding several large worktables and tools that Rob recognised as a wood lathe, chop saw and a belt sander. A variety of electric and manual hand tools were neatly laid out on one table. Overhead, strung from the rafters, were a series of hoses like elephant trunks which were part of the dust extraction system. Wooden bowls, Mitch's consumer stock, filled the wall shelves. One was still on the lathe waiting to be finished. What struck Rob was just how clean and tidy this shop was. Like Mitch.

"This cost me everything I had. And it's everything I have, other than the house and my truck. Everything I make from selling those bowls to the tourists or trading for food goes to cover expenses." Mitch stared at the floor, looking vulnerable. "For some reason I thought you should know that."

"You have everything you need."

"Not quite everything," he said in an injured tone. "Now, let me show you something I'm working on." He moved to the back of the shop and stopped at a large tarpaulin-covered object. "I told you that I used to work in marble when I was in college. I was pretty good. People mainly, busts and hands—my favourite was one of two elderly hands clasping. I was able to capture the love of two old people in those hands, and the fear of parting, but the one thing I found was that the marble always felt cold. The people always seemed real in some ways but lacking in…life. No matter how good they were, how much people praised them, I never felt I could bring them to life. Until now."

Mitch slid the tarp off, unveiling a full-sized male nude carved out of wood. It wasn't one of those chainsaw-carved folk-art pieces Rob had seen in small towns across the country. This was as detailed as any classical Greek sculpture and it seemed alive. Its skin of warm wood shone like it was sweating, and a body like this, all taut muscles and strained ligaments and tendons, would have sweated. Its arms were lifted forward, palms up, as if waiting to catch…something.

"Meet Eric," Mitch said.

"He's…beautiful isn't a strong enough word. He's a god."

"Actually, he's a neighbour. A construction worker, hence the physique—he built Aunt Sarah's house. That's how we first met. I stained the wood just slightly to give it that chestnut colour."

"Gorgeous," Rob said as he circled the sculpture, staring—its abs, its bubble butt, its penis. He suspected the real Eric would have been as hard as this one.

"Yes, you can touch it."

Rob ran his hands over the statue.

"Close your eyes while you do it." Rob did.

"Feel the warmth of the wood," Mitch instructed.

The sculpture was alive. He was touching the living Eric. He wanted to touch the real Eric. He could imagine the form breathing.

"Do you see what I mean? It's not like cold marble. Marble never lived. But when you carve wood, the life it once had somehow…returns."

Rob opened his eyes and saw Mitch before him, naked. His well-worked muscles, glistening with sweat, were accentuated by the light flooding in through the windows. His chest was dusted with black hair, his shoulders and biceps were strong and firm, and the shape of his ass was perfectly round like someone had implanted bowls under his skin. He stood there like Da Vinci's perfect man, if Da Vinci had given his man an erection. Rob took it into his hand.

"I thought you said this place could be hazardous to these."

"Well, normally yes, but I put all of the sharp tools out of the way."

Rob lowered Mitch onto the canvas that had covered the sculpture and began to caress, to taste, to consume him, starting with the toes and working up. He gorged himself on Mitch's testicles, choked himself on his cock. He felt the urge to turn this into a pagan ritual by devouring this sacrifice, then giving himself up to it. Rob stripped and mounted Mitch, impaling himself on his erection, now slick with saliva and Mitch's own fluids. Sweat poured from him as he rode Mitch's shaft. He had never wanted to be part of someone as much as he did at this moment. He was giving a part of himself that he hadn't given to anyone since Kevin, and nothing seemed more right.

Mitch thrashed in ecstasy as Rob caressed his nipples, then howled as he orgasmed. After his breathing returned to normal, he raised up his face to Rob's, and kissed him deeply as he turned the two of them until Rob was lying on the table, then Mitch took Rob's erection in his mouth and brought him to a rapid climax.

They lay on the work canvas, warmed by the late-afternoon sun. The sculpture of Eric looked down on them.

"Please tell me you've tried that?" Rob asked, pointing to Eric.

"Wouldn't you like to see the video?"

"There's a video?"
"Shut up and kiss me."
And Rob obeyed.

Chapter Nine

They got out of the large shower and Rob said, "Tonight I make dinner."

"Well, let's just see how you do and whether I keep you around," Mitch teased.

"I thought I'd already proven my usefulness."

Mitch smiled and said, "Well, something more can always be said for the multi-talented male."

As the lamb was marinating, Rob began to make notes on the day's activities, thoughts which could be used as the basis for the article.

I have spent the whole of my professional life travelling to the far-reaching corners of the Earth in search of adventure, a decade and a half of travelling to, what for me, were exotic places, and I have just learned something – every place is exotic if you don't live there. Exoticism is perceived as a function of distance – the farther we travel to obtain something, the more alluring the prize. We forget that what we find in our own backyard is exotic to someone halfway around the globe.

After dinner, they sat on the porch and watched the light of the setting sun play on the distant shore of the mainland.

"So—did I pass the cooking test?"

"Not bad. Not bad at all," Mitch said after giving it some consideration. "You do know how to handle meat. I give you nine out of ten."

"Just a nine?"

"If I gave you a ten, you'd stop trying to push yourself. I don't believe in tens."

"Good sensible answer," Rob said, wondering how to broach the big topic. "So, this article…it might take a while to write. I still have a lot of research to do. Would you mind if I stayed around for a while longer?"

Rob found himself growing anxious. Why wasn't Mitch answering? For the first time in twenty years, he had fallen for someone and he didn't want it to end. Mitch was kind, considerate, passionate and seemed in touch with himself. Was it too soon to feel this way about someone? Hadn't Rob's friends Todd and Steve moved in with each other after two dates, and they'd been together now for what, fifteen years? *Did I scare him off with the question?*

"I hoped you'd say something like that."

"You did? Then is that a yes?"

"What do you think?" Mitch had a sly smile on his lips.

"I have no idea right now. I know what I'd like you to say…"

"Of course it's a yes. It's a thousand yeses."

They kissed. It was becoming a habit neither one wanted to break.

The temperature dipped lower that night than it had in a while. Mitch lit a fire and the two snuggled up on the couch in front of it. They sipped on a hearty cabernet sauvignon—*"This one's imported from the faraway Okanagan Valley"*—There was a rustling outside.

"That'll be Rufus. He always likes a good fire."

Mitch got up and let the dog in. The dog, that is, and the horrible stench that followed.

"What the hell is that smell?" Rob managed to choke out.

"I...oh God, I'm gonna be sick." Mitch ran to the bathroom and Rob could hear him retching.

Mitch re-entered the room.

"You wuss," Rob said with a smile.

"I can't help it. I've got this thing with smells. Oh God!" Mitch ran back to the bathroom.

"Don't worry. I'll get this," Rob yelled out to Mitch. "You," he said to Rufus, "come here." He opened the door and told the dog to wait on the porch, which he did. Rob went into the kitchen where he filled a bucket with warm water and dish soap.

Outside he led the dog away from the house and proceeded to scrub him down from nose to tail. Rufus whimpered slightly at the indignity of it all.

"Don't complain to me about this. I wasn't the one who rolled in... God, what did you get yourself into? I've smelled some rank things in my life, but nothing like this."

Several buckets of water later, followed by a good hosing down—which Rufus took to be a game, snapping at the water as Rob tried to rinse him off—and a brisk towelling off, the two re-entered the house, Rufus smelling much better, Rob less so. Mitch was on the couch, still a little worse for wear, as the dog trotted over and plunked himself in front of the fire.

"I'm going to have a quick shower. Be back in a few minutes."

When he returned, he looked at Mitch on the floor with the dog and smiled.

"What's that for?" asked Mitch.

"This. The perfect domestic portrait. A Boy and His Dog." He picked up his wineglass.

"Come join us. A Boy, His Boyfriend and His Dog has a better ring to it," Mitch said.

Rob took a deep breath. "You are fearless. You know that, don't you?"

"Why do you say that?"

"You say what you feel. I would have been terrified to use the boyfriend word."

"Why? Isn't that what you want?"

"Yes," Rob said hesitantly. "Yes!" he repeated with confidence. "I guess I would have just been afraid to say it in case I was wrong and I'd make a fool of myself."

"Listen to you. You climb mountains. You sailed solo around the world before you were thirty — and yes, I have read all your books, you do that when you're crushing on someone — and, from some of those scars on your body, I'm guessing you've seen some things that would have scared most of us to death. But here you're telling me you are afraid of calling me your boyfriend just in case you're wrong."

Rob plopped down beside him. "I'm sorry."

Mitch took him by the hands. "There's nothing to be sorry for," he said. "I think it's adorable. It proves you're real, and not some fictional macho character. But you never have to be afraid of me. Ever."

"Okay. I promise."

"So, tell me something about you, Mr Hanson. Something I haven't read in any of your books."

"Hm. Something you haven't read… My middle name is Walker. I'm the last of my family, if you don't count my sister."

"I never knew you had a sister. What's her name?" Mitch asked.

"Jessica."

"Jessica…I like it."

"She'd like you," Rob said. "She'd see you as a good influence on her wayward brother."

"Intelligent woman. What else?"

"I'm patient, persistent, pathologically goal-oriented."

Mitch nodded his head. "No surprise there."

"Oh, you're looking for surprises, are you? Well, in spite of what you might think, I haven't had sex with another man in almost two years. Lots of flirting, but no sex."

Mitch leaned in. "Well, I'm glad I broke you of that nasty habit."

"And I thank you for it," Rob said, then gave him a kiss. "I had sex with a woman once in South America when I was a teenager just to see what it was like."

"And?"

"It was nice…but there was something missing."

Rob reached down and stroked Mitch's crotch with the back of his index finger. Mitch purred.

"I've been afraid a few times in my life," Rob continued. "Never in the wilderness, though. In spite of what some people say, nature doesn't try to kill you. Oh, you can die out there easily enough, but nature isn't malicious. Out there you're just part of it. You're one with it. It's not like a human who can try and hurt you just for the sake of making you afraid or gaining power over you. The only times I've been afraid were in the city. One time out of sheer loneliness when I almost did something stupid to myself…another time when someone almost did something stupid to me."

Mitch squeezed his hand.

"Maybe what I'm afraid of is stupidity." Rob laughed. "Good thing I'm not a politician."

They both laughed.

"What do see in your future? For you? Where do you travel next?"

"Wow. Trying to get rid of me so soon?"

"That's not what I meant. But you are a traveller."

"I don't know. I don't like to stack up too many projects. I'd never finish anything if I did that. I've got this story to finish off — the one about this beautiful place. Then the Somalia piece. That'll take six months to a year."

"Why Somalia? I mean, do people really want to travel there?"

"You'd be surprised at where adrenaline junkies want to travel. I just try to keep them as safe as possible."

"Scariest place you've been?"

"Sniper alley, Sarajevo. I wrote an exposé on rich tourists paying to shoot innocent people from rooftops. Sick bastards, all of them."

"Fuck. I can see why you like our Peak."

"Nature is never sick like a person. The exact opposite. Whenever I feel people-overload I have to get out into the wild. The tension just pours off me."

"Then where to next…to save your soul?"

"There's one hike I'm dying to try. The length of the Grand Canyon. Two hundred and seventy-seven miles along the river—over seven hundred and forty-five by trail, or what there is of it. If ever there was a holy place on earth, it would be there. Did you know that over four thousand people have summited Everest? Two hundred and fifty people have completed the seventy-nine-hundred-mile-long triple crown of hiking made up of the Pacific Coast, Adirondack and Continental Divide trails. And only twelve men have walked on the moon—that's the same number as have completed the whole length of the canyon below the rim in one push. I want to be lucky thirteen."

With that, Mitch's phone rang. It was a turquoise phone with a bell and cord mounted on the kitchen wall. Another remnant of Aunt Sarah.

"Aren't you going to get that?"

"What, and miss this? I'd rather sit here with you."

"I'll be all right. It might be important."

"I carve bowls for a living. What kind of emergency could it be?" The phone kept ringing. "Okay, I'll get it."

Mitch walked into the kitchen and picked up the receiver.

"Hello?"

"Yeah, is Robert Hanson there by any chance?" asked the caller whose voice was racked with coughs.

"Just a second."

Mitch walked into the living room. "It's for you."

"For me? Are you sure? Who is it?"

"They didn't say. They were too busy coughing. I couldn't even tell if it was male or female."

Rob went to the kitchen and picked up the heavy receiver. "Rob Hanson speaking."

"Robert, sweetheart, how are you?"

"Estelle?"

"Of course it's me. Who else would track you down like this?"

"Why are you calling on this number? How did you even find me?" Rob asked, surprised.

"It wasn't easy, let me tell you. Your number isn't picking up. Do you even have service on that god-forsaken speck on the map?"

"No. The locals protested when they wanted to put up a cell tower. They held the tech crew hostage in the house I'm staying in."

"How nice," she said dryly. "Trust you to find trouble on a grain of sand in the ocean. Do you know how many hotels I had to phone trying to find you?"

"Estelle, there's only one hotel on the island."

"I know that now. The woman there said you'd checked out, but some guy named Mitch would be able to put me in touch with you. I asked if she had this guy's number and she said yes, but wouldn't give it to me for privacy reasons. When I told her she'd already given me his name, so how hard would it be to share his number, she hung up on me. Do you know how hard it is to track down someone with just a first name?"

"I can only imagine."

"It turns out it's not very hard. There are only about a hundred phones on that rock you're on, so I was able to track the guy down in a few minutes."

"Estelle, you are a genius."

"So, you want to let this genius know why she's getting visits from the RCMP?" she pressed.

"What?"

"They're hunting for you, Robert. What the hell are you doing out there?"

"Nothing they should be interested in. Are you sure this is on the up and up?" he asked.

"As up as it can get. They'd already interviewed that piano-playing couch-surfing friend of yours."

"Karen? Crap, I'd better give her a call. Thanks."

"No problem. Just make sure you get that article in to Cedric," she warned. "I'm seeing him next week and I want it to be worth my while."

Rob hung up.

Mitch looked concerned. "Is everything okay? You look worried."

"It was just my agent. Look, do you mind if I make a long-distance call?"

"Mi teléfono es su teléfono."

Rob dialled Karen's cell number.

She answered, "Karen Salter."

"Hey, Karen, it's me."

"Where the fuck are you calling from?"

"The other side of the world, kiddo." Then Rob lowered his voice. "Tell me, did you get any strange visitors asking about me?"

"You mean those fake cops? Don't worry about them. I already reported them."

Rob frowned. "To who?"

"The real cops."

"Who? Like the Metros?"

"Yeah," she scoffed. "At least they have uniforms. Not like these guys."

"Didn't they show you ID?" Rob asked, concerned.

"How many times have you seen police ID? Never, I bet, so how do you know if it's real or a couple of scammers are flashing you something they ran up on Photoshop?"

Rob took a moment to process what she'd said. "Okay, what I'm really curious about is why they wanted to see me."

"Something about a guy being killed in Somalia."

"They told you that?"

"I guess they figured I was your girlfriend or something and thought that might shock me into telling them where you were. Where the hell are you, by the way?"

"Never mind that. Do me a favour — when I hang up, erase the call log on your phone. Will you do that?"

"Robby, you're starting to scare me."

"Oh, you want me to scare you? I think I'm falling for someone. It feels...real."

Rob was nearly deafened by the scream on the other end of the line.

"I'll be in touch," he said, smiling as he hung up.

Rob came back in and sat beside Mitch and Rufus.

"Is everything okay?" Mitch put his arm around Rob's waist. "You're so tense."

"Just some new people wanting a piece of me."

"Well, they can't have any. I'm using all of you right now."

"I'm glad to hear it."

Rufus fussed about, trying to find a more comfortable position, and Rob took Mitch's hand in his as they both stared off into the fire.

* * * *

He lay there on the couch, surrounded by people he couldn't quite see. They were laughing and talking, but he couldn't make out a word.

"Hey, beautiful."

It was a man's voice, he thought. A body joined him on the couch, snuggling beside him, pushing him into the back cushions.

"You feeling any better?"

The person started stroking the side of Mitch's face.

"I've got just what you need to make you feel better."

Mitch tried to call out. "No. No. Not now," he tried to say. He begged the person, crying. He wanted it to stop.

"No more!" Mitch yelled out.

Rob jumped out of a deep sleep to see Mitch, sitting upright in bed, soaked in sweat, yelling into the darkness.

"Hey," Rob said softly, hoping not to startle him. "Hey. Wake up." Rob reached out to rub his back. Mitch gasped and spun around, looking at Rob but not seeing him. He was gasping for breath.

"Wha…?"

"You were having a nightmare, but you're safe now. I'll protect you."

Mitch collapsed. Rob put his arm around him. He could feel his heart pounding.

"What were you dreaming about?"

Mitch said, "I…don't remember. There was this guy. I've dreamt about him before. I think he was trying to kill me."

Chapter Ten

It was pitch black outside, a good time to sleep, which was what Rob was doing until a hand touched his shoulder.

"Pssst. Time to get up." Mitch spoke softly.

"Wha? Is it time to go to the airport? The driver hasn't called yet, has he?"

"Okay, you've had enough time," Mitch said as he flicked on the light, then swatted Rob with the pillow.

"Up you get!"

"What time is it?"

"Four a.m."

"Four?" Rob was sliding out of the bed trying to steady himself. "We only got to bed a few hours ago."

"The solstice waits for no man. Even the mighty *you*. Now get dressed. I'll meet you at the truck."

"What the fuck?"

Rob stumbled around putting on his clothes from last night or, more precisely, from earlier that morning. Rufus looked on as Rob struggled to get on one of his socks.

"What are you staring at? I'd like to see you put on socks."

Rufus snorted and left the room.

Rob stumbled into the kitchen once he was dressed. "No coffee? Why is there no coffee?" he whined like a five-year-old. "Mitch? Mitch?"

Rufus barked at the open front door and walked outside. Rob obediently followed. Mitch was in the truck, waving a thermos of coffee at him. "Here, boy. Come get it."

"Very funny," said Rob as he tripped over a tree root, just catching himself. Mitch laughed and Rufus, now in the truck, barked and bounced around in the front seat.

A now even grouchier Rob opened the passenger door. "Back seat. Now!" Rufus moved without question.

"Morning, honey. This is for you," he said, passing him the coffee. "And these" — he passed him a box full of scones — "are for later."

"Do not tell me you baked these this morning."

"Okay. I won't." Mitch started the truck, threw it into gear and took off.

"Can I have one of these now?" Rob asked, referring to the scones.

"No. They're for sharing."

They drove on in silence before Rob asked, "Do you want to talk about your dream last night?"

Mitch stared straight ahead. "Nope."

Rob finished his last sip of coffee. "Okay." Rob changed the subject. "So, where are we going, and why now? The little forest animals aren't even up yet."

"It's Solstice Day."

"Okay."

"It's a big day on the island and I think you need to experience it. And keep your hands off the scones."

"Spoilsport."

They drove on through the morning darkness, a blackness amplified by the tree-canopied road, until they came out into a field. There were already a few cars there. Rob stumbled out of the truck and looked up at the predawn sky. He looked up. "Oh my God. Have you ever seen so many stars in one place?"

"Now go and drop the scones off on the table over there. I'm going to look for Maggie."

Rob made his way to a table which was illuminated by a single candle in a jar. A woman in a flowing caftan was pouring herself a cup of something from a carafe. She looked like she'd stepped right out of a 1960s commune.

"I was told to put these here," Rob said.

"You must be Mitch's new friend. I'd recognise his scones anywhere," said the caftan lady. "Happy Solstice Day." She leaned over and kissed him on the cheek.

"And the same to you," he offered as he arranged the scones on a tray.

"I'm surprised a healthy man like you didn't eat most of those on the way over."

"Trust me—I tried."

"You must be starving. Try one of these," she said, offering a brownie from a tray in front of her. "I just baked them last night. They go great with the tea."

"I don't mind if I do." He downed one in a single bite, chewing as he poured himself a cup of the tea, which tasted earthy with a touch of lemon. After the caftan lady left, Rob knocked back the tea and a few more brownies and headed off to check out the event.

There was remarkably little light beyond the candle at the food table. He had to watch where he was walking. People were clustered in small groups, many with cups of strong coffee pressed under their noses. The lack of light made the stars even brighter. It wasn't the first time he'd been to a dark sky preserve, but familiarity never bred contempt when it came to the night sky. He sat down. His body felt jittery. *Too much sugar,* he thought.

He lay down and stared at the sky. The more he stared, the more stars he saw. It was like lengthening the exposure of a photograph. *My eyes are cameras... Click. Click. Click.* "Click, Click. Click." He giggled.

"Hey, are you okay down there?" a guy asked, after he'd almost stepped on him.

"Amazing. Come here." Rob patted the ground and the guy lay down beside him. "Now look up. You can see everything. The light from those stars is billions of years old. The stars it's coming from may not even exist anymore, and we wouldn't know it for, who knows — millions of years."

The guy beside him began to snore. Rob giggled. *I should wake him up so he doesn't miss anything,* he thought. Just then a huge wet tongue slobbered across his face. "Rufus! Rufie, old boy. Here, lie down and look at the stars with us." Rufus just sat there. "Rufus, this is my friend...sleeping-guy. Sleeping-guy, this is the best friend you could ever have, Rufus, but you probably already know him. Everybody does."

Rufus let out a bark. Just then Mitch strode up. "Good boy." Mitch rubbed the dog behind the ear. "Hey, where did you get to? I've been looking everywhere for you."

"Have you ever seen the stars look so...runny before? Hey! Lie down with us and watch the runny stars," Rob said patting the ground.

Mitch asked, "So, who's your friend here?"

"Friend? Oh yeah. I have no idea. He just sleeps here. Come—look up. Wow, they're all the colours of the rainbow now. I've never seen them do that before..."

"Has someone given you something to eat or drink?"

Rob smiled. "Huh?"

"Have you eaten or had anything to drink since you've been here?"

"Yeah. Yeah. Hippie lady gave me a brownie and a cup of tea. But don't tell her—I stole a few more brownies. Shhhhh."

"Okay, listen up," Mitch yelled out. "No more feeding the newbie or you'll be the one cleaning up after him, not me." He reached out and took Rob by the hand. "Come on, Dopey, up you get."

He hauled Rob up onto his feet. Rob threw his arms around him. "Oh, I love you sooo much." He spoke the word *so* as if it had as many O's in it as there were stars in the sky, and as he spoke, he spun around while looking up, slowly at first, then faster and faster. Mitch had to grab him before he fell over or knocked into the matronly figure approaching them.

"Where aaaare we?" Rob asked.

"Welcome to *Tobar Creag*, my home. I'm Maggie Tupman. You must be Robert." She gave him a big hug. "I've heard a great deal about you—but they've only been rumours, I'm sure. Now we'll find out the truth."

"Don't go spooking him, Maggie. He's had a few of Shirley's brownies and isn't too steady on his mental pins at the moment," Mitch said.

"I hope you saved some of those treats for me. Solstice Day isn't quite the same without them."

"Oh yeah." Rob laughed and gave Maggie another hug. "Lemme show you where they are." He began to pull her towards the table.

"Maybe in a bit, Robert, but first I have to rally the troops," she said. "Now, come on, people! The sun'll be showin' in the east soon. We must be ready for 5:11."

Mitch grabbed Rob's hand. "Come on. You'll love it." He pulled Rob along with him as the small crowd moved to the edge of the field which Rob now saw was a cliff overlooking the Salish Sea and the rising sun.

"Come on, Rufus. You don't want to miss this," Mitch yelled. The dog bounded out of the darkness and was greeted with cries of "Rufus!" "Come here, boy!" "Where have you been hiding yourself, fella?"

The light of the solstice-day sun was growing, and with it the ocean of stars overhead began to disappear and Rob felt sad. "They're all melting away." He reached up to grab as many as he could and stuff them into his pocket for later.

At this point, an older fellow with a great white beard lifted his fiddle to his chin and began to play a haunting refrain. The people continued to gather, with Maggie in front, as the sun crept up over the horizon. Maggie raised her hands to the sun and sang.

> "As the sun she rises, sweet Gaia,
> let your light shine on us all,
> and cleanse us with the warmth of your rays,
> the brightness of your love,

the radiance of your joy,
the shining of your hope.
Let your light shine on us
as the sun she rises, sweet Gaia.
Let your light shine on us all."

She lowered her arms and the robe she was wearing slipped from her shoulders and left her in all her beauty. Then others followed – young, and old, and everyone in between – baring themselves as she had done.

"Come on," said Mitch as he began to undress. The tempo of the music picked up. The fiddle was joined by recorders, and drums and chanting. Everyone began to dance.

"Sure." Rob stripped down and flung himself into the music. He was without self-awareness, free of all inhibitions.

"I told you he'd be good," hollered Maggie who danced with the fervour of a twenty-year-old, her glorious folds and curves swaying independently of each other. The collected worshippers, like modern-day druids, moved to the rhythms of the music until the sun was above the horizon, then many flopped onto the grass while others dressed and got on with their lives.

"Are you having fun?" Mitch asked Rob.

"This is wild. I wouldn't have missed this for anything."

"Where else could you say that you danced naked with the mayor?"

"Hey, look – isn't that sculpture guy?"

"Eric? Yeah, that's him. Well, I guess now is as good a time to meet him as any," Mitch said. "Eric," he yelled. "Come here. I want to introduce someone to you."

And Eric, in all of his naked glory, except for a garland of flowers around his head, wove through the crowd and came to Rob.

"Eric. I'd like you to meet my friend Rob."

"Pleased to meet you." He extended his hand and Rob just giggled and threw his arms around him in a big stoner hug and gave him a kiss.

"Crap, you feel just like your statue."

"A little less wooden, I hope."

"I don't know. Let's see." Rob separated from the model and looked down at his swelling penis. "Nope, pretty much the same."

"I'm sorry, he's a little...wrapped up in the moment," Mitch explained.

"And the drugs, it seems."

"I'd better get him dressed and back home."

"Hey — you should come by for dinner tonight," Rob yelled.

"Sounds good. Seven o'clock good for you?"

"Sounds great," Mitch said with a little less enthusiasm.

"See you guys then," Eric said as Rob threw his arms around him again and gave him a huge kiss.

"Bye bye!" He giggled. Then in a loud stage whisper he said, "My God, you could lose yourself in that gorrrrrgeous ass. Hey — I think I'll have another brownie."

"No. I think you've had enough."

"You're not mad at me, are you? You can't be mad at me. I danced for the suuuun!"

"How could I possibly be mad at a five-year-old? Now, into the truck. You can get dressed when we get home."

Chapter Eleven

They both slept late. Rob was the first to wake. It was after three in the afternoon before he opened his eyes. He lay there on his side and assessed his situation. His mouth felt as though it was filled with cotton and his brain with woollen socks. His breath tasted like...*What the hell happened this morning and what exactly was in the tea and brownies? Those tasty, tasty brownies.*

He listened. The room was filled with the strangest sound. He could see Mitch still asleep beside him. *How,* he thought, *can someone so attractive look so...not, when they sleep?* He'd not noticed it before. That being said, he'd never been the first up. Mitch's mouth was opened at a strange angle. Rob tried to shift his own jaw into that position but it wasn't possible. Drool trickled out of the downstream side of that delicious mouth. And his beautiful black hair — if it were possible, he'd swear every strand was heading in a different direction. His eyelashes were the only things on his head that weren't in disarray. Rob hadn't noticed how long they were. Long and arched and black and...perfect. In short,

Mitch was even more adorable than before. But what was that smell? Just then his body was shoved forward into Mitch. Rob craned his head around to find himself face to face with Rufus' open maw, and his breath was…

"Oh God." The smell was worse than the night he'd come home after rolling in… Rob felt the gorge rise in his throat. He leapt over the dog and made it into the washroom just in time. Now he knew what Mitch had felt like the other night.

After rinsing and brushing his teeth, feeling mildly better, he returned to the bedroom to retrieve his clothes. Rufus was still under the sheets and now occupying most of the bed.

Out in the kitchen, Rob made a pot of coffee. If he were at home, he would have checked the papers online, checked his emails, checked his Twitter account and checked his Instagram by now. Here he felt no need, no desire to find out what anyone else was doing. The coffee was his only concern.

As he worked on his first cup and nibbled on a piece of dry toast, he wrote in his notebook.

It is too easy to come to false conclusions about a place when one only experiences what a general tourist book tells us to see. A true traveller, one who eschews the international hotel for a pensione and prefers street food to some posh café fare, knows that it is only when you immerse yourself in another culture that you can see it for what it truly is, for what the people are – not caricatures painted with wild eccentricities, but rather people who are living life by their own rules. I carry this thought with me wherever I go and if something seems out of place, the fault lies with me.

What might seem to some as a 1960s pseudo-sexual rite dressed up as a bizarre pagan ritual, akin to modern-day

*"Druid" performances, is, in fact, a beautiful shedding of
modern-day restrictions, one that celebrates humanity's part
in the natural world. I had, for the first time in many years,
abandoned the constraints placed on me by society, and
celebrated that simplest of joys – the fact that I was alive.*

"Good morning," Mitch said as he slid into the seat
across from Rob. His hair was perfect, face free from
drool. Gorgeous as ever. Somehow, he always
managed to have just enough facial hair, all neatly
trimmed.

"You look beautiful."

Mitch blushed.

"And it's almost evening, if you haven't noticed,"
Rob joked.

Mitch smiled and said, "Whatcha working on?"

"The article on the island."

"Can I see it?"

"Not yet. It's still too raw."

"Ooo. Sexy." Mitch winked at him.

Rob looked Mitch over and said, "I would love to
throw you on the table right now, but I need to put a
dent in this today."

"Well, you dent away and I'll start prepping
supper."

Rob replied, "The toast here is pretty good."

Mitch kissed him gently on the forehead. "Still a
little tender from this morning? I know just what you
need to pick you up. Roast chicken and veg. Don't
forget, Eric is coming over at seven."

"I have a slight suspicion that I may have done
something embarrassing with that one."

"You mean other than molesting him at the solstice
party?"

"Yeah. That's the way I vaguely remember it. Would *sorry* help?"

"You'll have to ask him now, won't you?" Mitch replied with a smirk.

"You're loving this, aren't you?"

"Oh, yeah. You better believe it. I thought for a minute I might lose you to him."

Rob paused, then said, "Did you have a...thing with him?"

Mitch looked at Rob.

"Would it make any difference?"

"We've all had lives before this one."

"Eric and I met when I moved here to help my aunt. I took one look at him and fell deeply in lust. We slept together for about six months — the time it took him to finish his work — and then, that was it. We both knew it. There were no hard feelings. No broken hearts. We're just friends now. No benefits."

"Thank you for telling me."

"Do you believe me?"

Rob stared him in his beautiful eyes and peered into his soul. "Yes. Yes, I do."

Mitch bent over and kissed him. "Now, get to work. You have a whole island to write about."

* * * *

Mitch prepared the dinner. Like most things he cooked, it was simple, yet Rob knew it would burst with flavour.

At a few minutes after seven, in island fashion, the door opened and Eric entered unasked. He was wearing khakis, a loose-fitting cotton shirt and sandals. As casually fitting as everything was, Rob couldn't help but make out the musculature that lay below. His cock stirred to attention on cue. Luckily, his untucked shirt hid the treasonous behaviour as he stood to shake Eric's hand.

"I want to start this evening off by offering my sincere apologies for my behaviour this morning."

Still holding his hand, Eric said, "Nothing to worry about. I've been on the receiving end of Shirley's laced baking before. They'll take down a pro."

Rob thought to himself, *How could anyone deny this, what — he'd be no more than thirty — this thirty-year-old god anything?* He then told his penis to behave itself.

Wine flowed freely that night, as did the conversation, providing Rob with the seeds that would help him weave stories of island politics, history and personal lives into a tidy story fit for publication. Rob learned about Eric's upbringing in Seattle, his life as a runaway, hitchhiking up to Vancouver, eventually making it to Marsh Island before he was twenty. He'd established himself as the go-to handyman of the island because he'd always been good with his hands. *And probably good on his knees*, Rob thought — knees which Eric kept rubbing up against Rob under the table.

As soon as Mitch had excused himself to go to the washroom, Eric slid his hand up Rob's leg and squeezed his cock through his pants. Rob jumped back, but his cock betrayed him, stiffening in seconds.

"I want this now. In my mouth or in my ass — your choice," Eric commanded.

Rob panicked. "I... He's coming back in a second. You can't. Not now."

"You're gonna finish what you started this morning."

"Look, as hot as this is — and it is super-hot — it's not gonna happen."

"We can let him watch," Eric whispered. "He always liked it when people watched. We can be doing it on the table when he gets back." Eric started to unbutton Rob's shirt.

"Oh, fuck..." Then, without thinking, Rob grabbed his full glass of red wine and threw it at Eric. It was like water on the wicked witch.

Mitch came back to Eric shouting and Rob mopping his shirt with a napkin. He was also working on Eric's pants with another hand, mainly to hide Eric's engorged penis from view, which only made matters worse.

"I am such a klutz," Rob yelled. "I am so sorry. I'll pay for the cleaning. I promise."

"I gotta go," Eric said as he twisted himself away from the table and stormed out, slamming the front door.

"But I made dessert," Mitch said sadly.

Rob finished mopping the wine off the floor, the chair, and the table. "I'm so sorry. I ruined everything. You went to so much trouble."

They both sat down to Mitch's apple pie and coffee. The evening had not gone as Rob had hoped and the impression he'd made on Mitch's friend was not exactly what he had planned. He just hoped that Mitch hadn't noticed anything.

As they were finishing the last of the wine, Mitch asked, "Did anything happen that you want to tell me about?"

Rob's face began to flush.

"I knew it. I knew it! You think I'd have learned by now. You can't trust that guy."

"Believe me. Nothing happened."

Mitch shook his head. "He'll try to sleep with any good-looking guy that crosses his path."

"So, it had nothing to do with me groping him in the park?" Rob asked.

"No. He'd have run into you eventually, clothes on or off, and made his move."

Rob leaned back in his chair. "How did you know? I thought I'd covered pretty well."

"A guy like Eric rarely gets a hard-on when his clothes have been doused in wine."

"You noticed that?"

Mitch smiled. "You might have big hands, but you'd need a frying pan to cover that python."

They both started to laugh. Rob slid one of the paper napkins off the table.

"If Eric's such a dick, why did you invite him over?" Rob asked.

"Me? You were the one who asked him."

"Oh. I'm sorry. You should have said something. I could have made up some sort of excuse…"

"No," Mitch began, now looking somewhat embarrassed. "It's my problem, not yours. Maybe I just wanted to show you that I wasn't a total geek and I *could* get a guy like that."

Rob looked deep into his eyes. "You are amazing. You know that, don't you?" Rob said.

Mitch's eyes began to tear up.

"You've done such a beautiful job of making me feel at home here, making me feel loved, and for forgiving me for being such an ass this morning. I was planning on picking you up some flowers for tonight, but I got so wrapped up in work… It was selfish. I hope this can make up a little bit for that," Rob said, pulling a paper flower he had quickly fashioned out of the folded, torn and twisted paper napkin from underneath the table. He presented it to Mitch, who cried even harder.

"It's a flower," Rob said helpfully.

"I know it's a flower, you idiot. It's the most beautiful flower I've ever seen."

They kissed over the table.

The phone rang.

"If it's that asshole, I'll rip his dick off," snapped Mitch as he picked up the phone. "You'd fucking well better be calling to apologise." Mitch gasped and covered the receiver, passing it to Rob. "It's that guy who called the other night," he whispered.

"What guy?"

"Your agent."

Rob took the phone.

"Hello, *Estelle.*"

Mitch burst out laughing. "It's a woman?"

Rob stifled his laughter as he playfully slapped him. "Shh."

"Sorry, Estelle. One of the neighbourhood kids was acting up. Now, what news do you have for me?"

"It's not good, Robert. They aren't going away. Someone is trying to implicate you in a shooting. It seems they don't take kindly to murders of citizens by rich foreign nationals."

"Rich foreign nationals?"

Mitch sat and stared at Rob, trying to pick up on what was happening.

"I think some local warlord is just looking for a pay-out," Rob answered in a lighter tone.

"It's not just the Somalis that are turning up the heat. It's our side. In case you haven't noticed, Canada's looking for a seat on the UN Security Council. It's been in all the papers. Probably even some out where you are. The Feds are none too happy with publicity like this." Estelle went into a coughing fit before continuing. "You've gotta get in touch with the Mounties right away and find out exactly what they want to know."

"Of course, you're right. You wouldn't happen to have an address for me?"

"Me not be one step ahead of you? You insult me. The guy trying to reach you is a Marc Robichaud from the RCMP Liaison Office. They said he works with the IOB, whatever that is. The nearest RCMP detachment is just over on Gabriola Island. 525 South Road. There'll be signs on the highway, if they have highways out there. In the meantime, I called your lawyers and don't argue about it. It's in your contract with your book publisher."

"Thanks for all this, Estelle. I'll pay them a visit tomorrow and I'll give the lawyers a call when I find out more. I'll fill you in as soon as I can."

Rob hung up the phone. Mitch was watching him, reading the lines in his face.

"Are you okay?" Mitch asked.

"Oh, hell yeah. Don't worry about it."

"Talk of lawyers tends to lead me to worry."

"Lawyers are just a precaution. My publisher feels better if they can hide behind a wall of them." Rob smiled, trying to take the edge off the situation.

Mitch looked concerned. "Why would they want to hide?"

"There are parts of the world where people make a living trying to get money out of tourists. Even crazy ones like me. Look, Estelle wants me to go and talk to a guy tomorrow. He's just over on Gabriola, so that's easy."

"The lawyer?"

Rob had to think fast. The last thing he wanted was for Mitch to think he was involved in a murder case. It was a short step from that to smuggling and drug cartels, given he was a guy who spent his life travelling. Not what someone like Mitch would be looking for in a husband. *Husband?*

"Lawyers are multi-armed beasts with tentacles everywhere," he said, running his hands over Mitch's chest. "I'll get the guy to fill me in on what these assholes want and we can figure out the best tactic to take."

"Has this ever happened to you before?"

"All the time. I had a guy once—he was my bodyguard, if you can believe it—he held my camera, passport and notes hostage until I agreed to pay for his kid's tuition. I just about shit myself until I found out it was for a local school and amounted to about eighty dollars." They laughed and Rob felt calmer letting Mitch believe the little lie he had told.

"Let's finish our dessert and head off to bed," Rob said. Then he whispered into Mitch's ear, "I'll show you a trick I know that Eric will never have a chance to see."

Chapter Twelve

Rob headed out first thing in the morning. He was greatly relieved when he found out that, as much as Mitch wanted to come with him for support, he had to attend an emergency island rate-payers meeting—something about a developer—and he needed to be there for quorum. Rob promised to call him from his cell phone as soon as he was heading back. Apparently, the fine citizens of Gabriola Island hadn't held *their* cell-tower technicians hostage.

He made it just in time to catch the ferry. Frances waved him on board along with a truck full of chickens. She was friendlier towards him than last time.

"So...I see you found Mitch okay at the market."

"Yes, and thanks for the connection."

"So...everythin' workin' all right over there?"

"Very well, thanks."

"So...are y'all done over there doin' whatcher doin'?"

"No, I just have to meet someone on Gabriola. Business. I'll be on the four o'clock ferry back."

"Good. Glad to hear it. I'll save room for you."

"Gee, that's nice of you. Say — do you know how to get to South Road from the ferry dock?"

"You bet. Just head straight on Malaspina Drive and hang a right on Taylor Bay which turns into South Road. You can't miss it. Just look for the signs pointing to the RCMP."

Was her comment about the RCMP a coincidence? he wondered. She would have no reason to suspect anything, would she? Rob guessed that when it came to Mitch, Frances suspected everything.

* * * *

Rob found the detachment easily. He pulled into the parking lot in front of the single-storey brown clapboard structure. It was a surprisingly unimposing station given that it was the seat of law enforcement on the island and the representative of a national police force with a large international reputation.

He hopped out of the Jeep, then approached the main entrance and its oxidised aluminium screen door. The whole thing was quaint, but experience had taught him one thing — quaint could be dangerous.

The inside of the detachment building was pretty much a reflection of the outside — rustic panelled walls, a drop ceiling of aged once-white tiles and a laminate counter complete with a homemade pottery bowl filled with wrapped candy. The office seemed empty. He stood there a moment just in case someone was out back doing something they would prefer to finish uninterrupted.

Rob wasn't nervous about what might happen. He was rarely nervous when it came to meeting people of power. Cautious, yes—to be otherwise could be lethal—but showing nerves to a person of power was like being afraid of a dog. The dog always knew it.

He had been there a minute and decided to ring the bell. The moment he did, a young woman came around the corner blowing on a steaming cup of something.

"Sorry to keep you. Just heating up lunch."

"A little early, isn't it?" he joked.

"Not when your shift starts at five." She smiled at him. "So, what can I do for you? Directions? Fishing permit? Report a lost dog?"

"Nothing so normal, I'm afraid. My name is Robert Walker Hanson. I think you might be looking for me."

"Sir, if that's a come-on line, I've heard better," she said, still smiling. This Corporal Evans—as the name plate on the desk identified her—was good.

"No, I mean it. I had a call from someone who told me a Liaison Officer named Marc Robichaud from the IOB, whatever that is, was trying to find me."

Rob figured playing innocent would be the best tactic. He knew what the IOB was—the International Operations Branch—the arm of the RCMP that dealt with crimes and threats from abroad. The Liaison Officer was responsible for the exchange of criminal intelligence, especially in matters of national security with other countries, and provided assistance with investigations which directly affected Canada. If this was about what he thought it was, this man Robichaud would be working out of the RCMP's Dubai office.

"Well, that's a bit different than looking for a lost dog. Where's this friend that was contacted by Mr Robichaud?"

Give her as much information as possible, he thought. *Better to be too helpful.*

"There were two friends, actually. My agent, Estelle Fillion, and Karen Salter, who is taking care of my house. Both are in Toronto. Would you like their contact info?"

"Yeah. Thanks. If you could just write their names and numbers on this, that would be great." She slid him a paper and pen. "So, you have an agent. Are you an actor?"

"Worse," he said, sliding the pen and paper with the names and numbers back to her. "I'm a writer."

"I didn't know writers had agents."

"We need all the help we can get." *Good. I made her laugh.*

"Let me see what I can find out. Why don't you have a seat."

Rob took the seat and Corporal Evans went to a desk and ran a few searches on her computer, then made a call. She spoke quietly to the other party, glancing up at him from time to time. He couldn't tell where this was going. She hung up the phone and returned to the counter. Rob joined her.

"Do you travel much, Mr Hanson?"

"A fair bit, yes. I'm a travel writer. I'm writing a piece on Marsh Island right now."

"Nice place. I was there once on a holiday," she commented. "Have you travelled abroad lately?"

"Just got back from Somalia about a month ago."

"That'll be it then. You're going to have to talk to one of my superiors about some questions Mr Robichaud has."

Rob frowned. "Won't I be talking to him personally?"

"I doubt it. He's in Dubai."

"Oh. Am I in some kind of trouble?" *Keep it dumb and innocent. A Canadian who has been linked to a dead guy in the streets of Mogadishu is going to be in trouble.*

"Did you see anything unusual during your last trip?" she continued.

"In Mogadishu, everything is strange by our standards."

"I guess so." She paused for a moment. "Look, it's probably not as bad as you might think. Here's my superior's name and number in Victoria. He might be able to clear this up with a phone call."

"Can I call him right now?"

"Sorry, but he just left here about an hour ago. It'll be a while before he gets to Victoria. I'd try him tomorrow after nine. He works a decent shift."

"I'll do that. Thank you." Rob stood, and shook her hand.

"Care for a candy?" Corporal Evans indicated the candy dish.

"Don't mind if I do." Rob took one and headed back out into the parking lot. He called Mitch and got his voicemail. "Hey. Just wrapped up my meeting and I'm going to head back on the next ferry. I think I might take your advice and drop by for a talk with Sheila Marsh on my way home. That should give me what I need to finish the article. See you soon."

Rob got into his Jeep and started the engine. He might be able to catch the earlier ferry back if he hurried. He pulled out onto South Road and headed to the dock. As he drove, a car followed at a distance.

"Huh. Now I wonder what he was doin' there?" Francis said to himself. He'd have to ask his wife. She would have talked to him on the crossing over. He drove on, keeping his distance. *Not much reason for him to be makin' a trip just to see them,* he thought. *Well, if a man is tryin' to keep a secret, 'specially from my wife, it won't be a secret for long. That woman can't bear not knowin' everything about everyone.*

* * * *

Rob hadn't taken this route since the day he had met Mitch, the time when Sheila had spoken with him at the cemetery — the day after she'd almost run him over. It seemed like a lifetime ago. It was a short drive along the tree-canopied lane before Rob turned into the long driveway leading to Marsh Island Veterinary Clinic. The sign was emblazoned with a cartoon dog, cat and... He wasn't too sure what. A weasel, maybe. Or a snake.

Rob found Sheila at the front door talking to a young boy who was holding a small kitten that seemed to have been through the wars.

"Now, Tigger got off pretty lightly this time, but you're going to have to promise me you'll keep him inside from now on. Okay? Next time he might not be as lucky."

"Yes, Dr Marsh. I promise," he said, holding on to the kitten and looking up to the heavens as he carefully made his way to a waiting car.

Rob grinned. "That one looks a little worse for wear."

"The boy or the cat?"

"Both, I guess," Rob answered.

Sheila shook her head in amazement. "Got carried away by a golden eagle from the sounds of it. The cat, that is. Not the boy. Saved in the nick of time by the boy's sister who threw a rock at it as it flew off. Tigger's lucky she's as good a shot as she is. The bird dropped the poor little cat into a tree where they were able to retrieve it."

"Now that's a great story."

"So, what can I do for you?" Sheila asked. "You don't seem to have any injured animals on you, unless there's one in your car."

"No, I've come burdened with questions, not injured kittens. Rob Hanson," he said, extending his hand.

"I remember you. Taking pictures, as I recall."

"Yeah. Just down the road where you kindly didn't run me down. Then later in the cemetery. An appropriate reminder of what can happen if I don't pay attention. I'm writing a piece on Marsh Island for a magazine. Mitch Carcross told me that you're the go-to person when it comes to local history."

"Well, most of the local history is my family's history, so I guess I am."

"Do you have a minute to talk? I like to put things in a historical context and there's really not much written about the island."

"No, I don't suppose there is," she agreed.

"You can check with Mitch if you're looking for references."

"No, Mitch has already vouched for you by taking you in."

"Oh?" Rob looked surprised.

"Word spreads fast on a small island. Especially when it concerns one of our favourite sons." She looked him in the eye for a moment. "I sense that you came to this island searching for one thing and found something more than you expected."

"You can say that again."

"I'm glad. So, how long will you be staying with us?"

Rob smiled. "Why do I have a feeling that I'm the one being interviewed instead of the other way around?"

"Oh, I've only just begun."

Sheila headed back into the clinic. Rob wasn't sure if he was meant to follow until she held the door for him. "Are you coming?"

She poured them both coffees and settled into one of the waiting room chairs. *Not comfortable enough to encourage a long stay,* Rob thought.

"So, what do you want to know?" Sheila asked.

To Rob's surprise, they talked for the better part of two hours. For such a small island, it had enough history for a book, let alone an article. Rob took several pages of notes.

"I like that you're old school. No recorder, no videoing with your phone," she said.

"I prefer to listen and try to understand. I trust my brain more than a machine. Technology has a bad habit of failing you at the worst possible time."

"Trust is an important trait, whether in people or equipment."

He sensed she was going somewhere with this.

"Can I be honest with you?" she asked. "More to the point, can I trust you with something? Trust you to keep it to yourself?"

"I can't promise not to write something if I don't know what it is."

"Oh, it has nothing to do with your article. Or I hope it doesn't. It has to do with Mitch."

"Oh?"

"I've seen you together. I can tell you're smitten," she said. Rob looked at her, not wanting to give too much away. "I saw the two of you in action at Maggie's Solstice Day party. Don't worry. As I recall, at my first party, I had to be removed from a tree that I was deep in conversation with." She looked deeply into his eyes for a moment. "What do you know of Mitch's time before he came to the island?"

Rob weighed his words carefully. "I knew him as a kid. I was best friends with his brother. After I'd finished college, I had some personal issues to deal with and we all went our separate ways. Until we met here."

"What I'm going to tell you, I do, not as a gossip, but because I love that boy as a son. Swear you'll keep it to yourself."

Rob's heart beat a little faster. He closed his notebook and said, "I understand. I promise."

"After Mitch went to college, that was after his folks died, he became the toast of the school. He was brilliant, talented, handsome — the picture of success. He led a charmed life until he met a guy who got him hooked on drugs. It nearly destroyed him.

"It was at that point that his Aunt Sarah adopted him. I mean, actually adopted him. She brought him over here to get him away from that evil man, away from the drugs and the pressure the college was putting on him. We all protected him. Francis and Frances kept an eye on everyone who was coming to the island, and on several occasions refused passage to someone they thought might be that guy.

"He had good times and bad, sometimes sinking so low he'd disappear for days on end. Once, early on, he'd been gone for weeks. We knew he hadn't taken the ferry off the island, and he couldn't have swum off. He was always shit in the water. Sarah was at her wit's end. She figured he'd drowned or something. Turned out whenever he was at his lowest, he'd escape to the Peak. Sometimes he'd hide out in a small cave he'd come across. I found out later from him that he'd been living off plants and bugs and spring water. A voice had come to him in a dream and told him what to eat and what to avoid. Crap, there are lifelong woodsmen out there who've died eating the wrong berry and this kid from the city survived.

"I found him out there on the highest rock once, sitting cross-legged like a guru from India, just staring out at the sea. On his face was the most angelic look of peace. It took him a moment to acknowledge me. He smiled and said 'I'm going to be okay, Sheila. The mountain has transplanted part of its soul into me.' I was sure he must have been on something, but he stood up, took my hand and led me back to where I left my car. The only other thing he said was 'Don't worry. Everything is going to be okay.'

"The people of Marsh Island helped him live and, when Sarah died, helped him survive, and in turn, he has taken personal responsibility for everyone on this island, and the island itself.

"I ask you to keep this in mind, body and soul in your relationship with that boy. Do anything to violate his trust and you will have to deal with each one of the residents of this island. Do you understand?"

"Yes. I do. And I promise I won't hurt him."

"Good. The inquisition is now over. And if Mitch ever finds out that we had this conversation, I will euthanise you faster than a sick old dog."

* * * *

Rob walked through the door. Mitch was standing at the kitchen counter washing up some dishes.

"Hey handsome," Rob said as he wrapped his arms around Mitch from the rear. Mitch's hands were still in the dishwater. "Got you just the way I like you. Helpless." Their heads twisted as they kissed.

Rob noticed something was wrong. "Hey. Are you all right? You're so tense."

"I'll be all right. Just..."

"The meeting. How did it go?" Rob asked.

"We're doing battle with a big developer from Victoria. Somehow they managed to convince the province to support a bid to build a resort on Admiral's Peak."

"What? How can they do that? Isn't it protected?"

"You only protect what you think's at risk. It was Crown land. No one thought anyone would be interested in it. We're a small island that no one ever comes to and now they want to build *that*." Mitch nodded towards a pamphlet on the counter.

It was a well-produced brochure promoting Admiral's Peak, a boutique lodge of one hundred rooms, with spa, gourmet restaurant and health club. A development project that would create one hundred and fifty new jobs and bring prosperity to this small, unexploited jewel of the Salish Sea.

"They're going to destroy the island and hand it over to the rich." Mitch was on the verge of tears. "My beautiful mountain — they're going to rape it. Bulldoze what makes it precious and turn it into a fucking theme park!"

Rob held him. Mitch's hands dripped soapy dishwater down his pants. Rob wiped away the tears.

"There's something else," Mitch added.

"Oh?" If he'd believed in a god, Rob would have prayed that it had nothing to do with the RCMP. He'd avoided telling Mitch he'd been part of something that resulted in the death of a man. Just then he heard the washroom door open and the sound of the toilet refilling. A man walked into the room.

"Hey, Robby. What a small fuckin' world."

There, before Rob, stood the one person that had almost ruined him.

"I guess you can imagine the surprise I had when I came here and found out you were seeing my baby brother. That's what it is, isn't it? You and him together, like you and me used to be? Sounds a bit...weird, don'tcha think? Almost kinky."

"That's enough, Kevin," Mitch snapped. "Rob didn't even recognise me when we met."

"But I bet you jumped him the moment you found out who he was, just to get back at me." Kevin's eyes burned into Rob.

"This has nothing to do with you," Rob said to Kevin. The age-old hurt bubbled back to the surface.

Kevin looked much older than his forty-five years. Booze, drugs or a combination of both had taken their toll on the once handsome face and hard-muscled body. He stood there, paunched stomach, creased face, stooped, looking more like he was sixty. He held on to the corner of the counter, balancing himself. *He's fucking drunk,* Rob thought.

"Okay. Okay. I'm sorry. I was just... I was really surprised when I found out. That's all. Wouldn't you be?"

Mitch conducted them into the living room. "Let's just sit and have a coffee and... I'll find us something to eat." He went back into the kitchen.

The two exes stared at each other like boxers sussing out an opponent.

"You're lookin' great. You work out?" Kevin asked.

"Yeah. I need to be in shape. For work."

"Huh." Kevin looked him up and down. "So whataya do?"

"Write." Rob wasn't in any mood to open up.

"I never thought of that as a physically demanding kinda job."

"It depends on where you do it."

"I suppose…"

They glared at each other in silence.

"So, you visit Mitch often?" Rob probed.

"Well, I like to see how the old homestead is holding up. Gotta make sure my assets are being well taken care of."

"Your assets?"

Mitch came back in with coffees and a plate of cookies.

"What—not homemade?" Kevin asked.

Rob moved over to sit beside Mitch and put his hand on his leg. "They're my favourites."

"Do you have anything harder than this?" Kevin asked, holding up his mug of coffee, which trembled in his hands. "I mean, it was a long haul getting over here."

"No," Mitch said.

"Oh. Right. I forgot," he replied, then to Rob added, "You gotta stay clean while you visit the queen."

Rob could see where this was going. "So…are you planning on staying long?"

"I was thinking a week."

"A week?" Rob said, surprised.

"Kevin usually stays here until he's…feeling better," Mitch explained.

"What he means is until I sober up."

Rob knew what he had to do to save Mitch. "Of course. You have to stay. You're family."

Rob put his arm around Mitch, thinking, *If you do anything to hurt this guy, so help me, I will kill you and they will never find your sorry-assed body.*

"So, how was your trip to Gabriola?" Mitch asked Rob.

"Let's not worry about that tonight."

Rob could tell that Mitch had had enough for one day. Telling him the truth would only make things worse. Rob looked at Kevin and heard the voice in his head say, *It's all going to slip away…just like before,* and he hoped that it wasn't true.

Chapter Thirteen

The next morning, Mitch stood in the kitchen making coffee. Whenever Kevin was around, which was far more often than he'd admitted to Rob, Mitch felt awkward, like he was in someone else's home. Kevin had always treated Mitch like he was being allowed to stay here out of his older brother's generosity. In his head, Mitch could almost hear his brother's voice. *"As the oldest, I should have been the one to inherit the house when that old bitch died! What did you do to brainwash her into hating me so much? And now you bring Rob into the picture, by sleeping with him. Is this some warped fantasy on your part?"*

"Coffee ready yet, sunshine?" Kevin said, walking into the kitchen. Mitch jumped, spilling coffee grounds on the floor. "Come on, you gotta learn to keep a cleaner house if you're planning on keeping Mr Hanson happy."

"I didn't hear you come in." Mitch got down on his knees and swept up the grounds.

"Take it easy. I was only joking."

"Yeah."

"Look, we've gotta have a talk before Prince Charming gets up. Brother to brother."

"Sure."

Kevin led Mitch out onto the porch and closed the door.

"I just want to give you a heads-up as to what you're getting yourself into here," Kevin said, putting his hand on his brother's shoulder. "I'm just trying to look out for you. That's what a big brother does."

"Okay."

"I care about you. You know that, don't you?"

"Sure." Mitch remained reserved.

"So, you know I wouldn't bullshit you, right?"

"Sure."

"I tell the truth cuz you're my brother and I love you, and the truth is...you can't trust that guy."

Mitch's face turned hot as he said, "No! You don't understand."

Kevin grabbed his brother by both shoulders. "No — I do understand. I've been there. I've seen him in action, and he can't be trusted. Before you say anything, I want you to think about it. Does he ever just dance around questions you have about him?"

"No, he's a very open person."

"Yeah, like when you asked him last night about his trip to Gabriola?" Mitch just stared at him. "Has he ever fooled around with another guy and just brushed it off, blaming it on the booze?" Kevin waited for a moment to give him time to think. "Has he ever offered to pay for things since he's been here?"

"He buys food sometimes..."

"Sometimes? Don't you see what's happening here? It's a pattern. He's using you like he used me in university. I spent most of my money covering his bar and restaurant tab. He has no money, so he trades his looks for room and board."

"No! That's not him. He's a writer, and a good one. He writes books that are sold — "

Kevin interrupted. "Do you realise that the average writer in this country makes less than ten thousand a year? Why the hell do you think I bailed on the business? Writing's for suckers. Hanson's nothing more than a middle-aged hustler and you're his john, and the sooner you realise that, the better off you'll be. Hopefully you'll wise up before he's finished draining you of everything you've got and dumps you for a younger guy with more to offer."

Mitch ran inside. He needed to make coffee before Rob got up. Needed? No. Wanted! He wasn't going to be manipulated by his brother. Mitch slammed around in the kitchen, putting out the coffee mugs, creamer and sugar. He stood there and stared at them, trying to calm the storm in his head. A hand on his shoulder startled him and, without thought, he spun around, hand balled into a fist ready to drill it into... Rob stood there, his face the picture of shock and fear.

"What happened? Are you all right?" Rob asked with concern.

Mitch was shaking. He threw his arms around Rob. "I am so sorry. I don't know what that was all about. You just startled me. That's all."

Staring into Rob's eyes, and safely in his arms, Mitch felt himself begin to relax. He sank down onto a kitchen bar stool.

"What happened?" Rob asked.

It was as if Rob had hypnotised him and he couldn't tell a lie. "I had a fight with Kevin. It happens every time he comes for a visit."

"Why do you let him stay? It's your house, isn't it?"

"Yes." *Why is he asking that?* "I told you, my aunt left it to me in her will," Mitch answered defensively.

Rob replied, "It's just that he said something about coming by to check out his asset."

"Kevin thinks Sarah should have left it to him, being the oldest. When he's had too much to drink, he sort of gets it in his mind that that's the way it is."

"If he has no claim on the house, then you can just tell him to leave," Rob reassured him.

"He's my brother."

Kevin came in from the porch. He smelled of cigarette smoke. "Coffee finally ready?"

"Yeah. I'll get it," Mitch said weakly.

Rob took control. "No. You guys sit down. I'll fix breakfast."

"Well," Kevin said. "It's been a long time since you served me breakfast. Does it still come with a little extra on the side?"

"Sorry, but this chef only works for one boss," Rob calmly replied, giving Mitch a kiss on the head.

"Well, times really have changed."

"Snap! Got me with that one, Kevie," said Rob, putting the coffees down on the table.

"So, Robby. I hear you were over on Gabriola. What takes you there?"

"Just seeing someone about a legal matter connected to a writing job."

"Writing? How long have you been doing that?"

"Gads…almost twenty years now?"

"Following in your old boyfriend's footsteps?"

"Not quite," Rob said, trying to keep the sarcasm to a minimum.

"So, does writing pay any better than in the old days?"

"God no. Some things never change. But things could be worse. I could be a poet." Kevin laughed at that. The first honest sound out of his mouth since he'd seen him.

"That was a standing joke we had in school," Kevin explained to his brother.

"So, what do you specialise in?" Kevin asked.

"Travel."

"Like those articles in airplane magazines?"

"If that's who's buying. Small magazines pay about four hundred unless you've got a name. Larger ones, four times that. I'm here writing a longer piece about Marsh Island."

"Huh. I guess you have to write a lot just to pay the bills."

"You should know by now that most writers don't make a great living on what they love to do."

Mitch could see what Kevin was doing, but Mitch didn't care if Rob made a lot of money writing. He had enough money to keep both of them…

Then a small spark went off in Mitch's brain, so small he barely noticed. Even in the dark. It was a spark of doubt, and a spark of doubt could easily cast a shadow of doubt. The small seed planted by his brother had begun to germinate.

* * * *

That evening, Mitch lay in bed. The curtains were drawn. Rob sat on the edge.

"I'm going to meet with someone tomorrow. I'm not sure if this will work but I think I know something that will help."

"With what?" So much had happened today that Mitch wasn't sure which problem Rob was talking about.

"With the fight against the developer."

"Oh, yeah. Sorry. Too many things rattling around my brain today."

"Don't worry. I'm here for you." Rob leaned over and kissed him, but Mitch didn't kiss back. "A good night's sleep will help. Come on. Scooch over." Mitch slid to his side of the bed and Rob got under the covers then turned off the bedside lamp.

"I have an idea about who could help in the development fight. I've got a meeting in Victoria with the magazine publisher. If I could get him on our side, we could get a ton of local publicity. That and what I can get from Twitter and Instagram, we can start a grassroots tsunami to blow those guys right off the island. Now, close your eyes and get some sleep." With that he put his arms around Mitch and drifted off to sleep. Mitch stared into the blackness and wondered. *Kevin can't be right. Can he? He's wrong about everything. But...*

Chapter Fourteen

Rob didn't think about contacting the RCMP while he was in Victoria. His priority was to meet with Cedric and get the weight of his magazine behind the Save Marsh Island campaign. He would give the Mounties a shout later.

Vancouver Island Publishing was a small operation in the 800 block of Broughton Street in Victoria, just on the east side of downtown. Rob had taken the first ferry off Marsh Island which allowed him to get the 7:35 a.m. ferry out of Descanso Bay on Gabriola to Nanaimo which would give him plenty of time to find street parking and make his 10:00 a.m. meeting with Cedric Craddock.

Rob bounded up the stairs to the second-floor office where he found a person who he assumed, from the position and configuration of her workspace and software running on her computer, was the receptionist/layout artist/editor and, quite possibly chief copywriter of *West Coast Travel* and other publications. She was hunched over her desk, alternating between her keyboard and a hand-scribbled manuscript, muttering to herself. Rob stood there for a few minutes before he cleared his throat. Her face shot up from her desk like a cornered animal. A strand of brown hair crossed her sweaty forehead.

"Sorry. I didn't mean to startle you," Rob said.

"My God, how long have you been standing there?" she replied, trying to tidy up her appearance. "I don't usually ramble on like that when there's a stranger looking on."

"No need to explain. I mumble to myself all the time." Rob never shied away from flirting when he was in a good mood — even with a woman. "Rob Hanson. I have a ten o'clock appointment with Mr Craddock."

"Ten o'clock?" She scrambled around her desk finally finding her day-planner which she proceeded to flip through. "Ten o'clock. Ten o'clock, ten o'clock, ten o'clock. What day is it?"

"Wednesday," Rob replied. She continued to stare at him. "The twenty-fourth. Of August."

"Right." She went back to the day-planner. "Here it is. August twenty-fourth, ten a.m.… Nope. Nothing here."

"But I spoke to him yesterday. I'm writing an article for him and I have a new angle I'd like to pitch."

"Oh. I don't doubt that you have an appointment. He's just forgotten to write anything down in the book, not that I should be surprised. He never does. But he's not in yet. He'll be getting his hair trimmed right about now. But don't worry, he doesn't have much hair so it won't take long. Can I get you a coffee?"

"Thanks. I'd love one."

She spun around to the counter behind her desk where she popped a pod into her Nespresso machine and in a few minutes presented Rob with a perfect coffee.

"The pay may not be the best, but the coffee's decent. My name's Brenda, by the way," she said with a flirtatious smile.

"Nice to meet you." He smiled, shook her hand and sat down to wait.

* * * *

Cedric Domenico Ferdinand Craddock was a vain man. He would spend an hour each morning shaving, trimming his nose and ear hairs and perfuming and primping his receding hair, all in the belief that he could maintain the looks he'd once had. His dressing routine would add another half-hour, if he'd remembered to polish his shoes the night before. That was not to say that he was an unattractive man, but at the age of sixty-five, it was looking more and more like the effort was not worth the result.

Every Wednesday, Cedric would head off to Enrico's for a trim. Enrico, his barber, who had been cutting men's hair for longer than Cedric had had any, insisted that the weekly visits were a waste of good money, but Cedric felt it was important to look his best at all times. The procedure took a matter of a few minutes and Cedric walked out of the shop twenty-five dollars poorer but feeling a million dollars richer.

He always stopped in at the same café on his way into work and the barista always knew what he wanted—a twenty-ounce, triple shot, one pump mocha, non-fat, no whip, with exactly four shakes of cinnamon stirred in. Woe betide the barista who shorted Cedric on his cinnamon shakes. For a straight male, he could out-hissy-fit any princess in Victoria.

Cedric never hurried to work. Punctuality was a sign of subservience and he was the boss. He arrived precisely at fifteen minutes past the hour — thirty minutes on Wednesdays. It never occurred to him that being precisely late every day was still being punctual. Brenda knew this but kept it as her own private joke.

At ten-thirty a.m., the door to Vancouver Island Publishing opened and Cedric made his entrance. He was shocked when he saw a young man standing there. Vancouver Island Publishing rarely had a visitor. In this electronic era, personal visits from anyone were an outdated event. The two men stood there and stared at each other for a moment.

"Mr Craddock, your ten a.m. appointment is here," Brenda announced.

"My…who are you?"

"Rob Hanson. Estelle Fillion's client."

"Oh my God, of course. It completely slipped my mind. Please, come into my office, Mr Hanson. Brenda, hold my calls." He led Rob into the inner office.

* * * *

The descent began with a knock on the door.

Mitch had been talking to Kevin over afternoon coffee in the kitchen. The kind of people who would visit Mitch never knocked. People in small communities didn't do that. It was a thing done in cities where people didn't know each other, and on the island, everyone knew everyone. So the sound of knocking at the door was entirely out of place. Mitch went silent for a moment until a second set of three raps shook him out of his stillness.

He opened the door to find a man and a woman dressed in suits. Another gross anomaly. He knew their type from his previous life.

"May I help you?" he asked as politely as possible but wasn't able to hide the subtle quaver in his voice.

"Rob Hanson?" asked the woman.

"No. Mitch Carcross."

"Does Mr Hanson live here?" she asked.

"Yes. He's staying here."

"Is he in?" questioned the man.

"No..." Mitch replied. His mind was filling with uncertainty. He knew something was wrong, but Rob must be okay or they wouldn't be asking for him.

"May we come in?" the woman said and started to enter without waiting for an answer.

"Who are you?" He remembered the last time something like this had happened. It was in Vancouver, and they weren't there for Rob.

"Well. This is interesting." It came from Kevin, who had a sly smile on his face.

* * * *

For a man as prim and proper as Cedric Craddock, Rob would have expected his office to be a little more organised and a lot cleaner. Rob was mistaken. Craddock was a publisher, and this was the sort of publisher's office that Rob was used to — piles of manila envelopes, containing manuscripts from hopeful writers; bundles of issues of magazines to be given away as promotional material; stacks of city guides; other publishers' output; coffee cups; and, much to his delight, an old Remington typewriter which sat beside an only slightly newer computer. It was clear that Brenda did the heavy lifting in this operation.

"So, Rob—you don't mind me calling you Rob, do you?" Cedric asked, indicating that Rob should sit.

"Not at all, Mr Craddock."

"Please, call me Cedric. Estelle would have my balls if I treated you any differently. Now, how is your piece for my magazine coming?"

"That's why I asked for this meeting."

"Oh?" Cedric replied with a shade of concern.

"No—I've finished writing the article for you. I think you'll be pleased with it. A little place like Marsh Island is such a gem that the article pretty well wrote itself."

"I'm pleased to hear that."

"But recent events have made me wish I'd written a different piece."

"What do you mean by recent events?" Cedric asked with concern.

"I've just discovered that there is a push to develop the island in a way that will destroy everything that makes it special. Its socio-eco-tourist resources could be pushed to the limit."

Cedric frowned. "What is that supposed to mean—in terms that a simple publisher might understand?"

Rob clarified. "Any destination can safely handle a certain number of tourists before the drain on the resources like drinking water, transportation, and space in general will cause the resources to run out. Think of what's happened to Venice, where Venetians can't afford to live in their own city because of the demands placed on the city by the cruise ship industry. Marsh Island is like a well-functioning ecosystem and, as such, is a finely balanced organism. If the developers want to add thousands of people a year to it, what they have now will collapse, and what the tourists went there for in the first place will be gone. The island community bio-system, as it now stands, will die."

"Well...that certainly is a statement. And what are you proposing?"

"The article begins" — Rob passed Cedric a USB key containing the manuscript and image files — "by covering the beauty of the place, its history and the people who make the island the colourful destination it is. It wraps with the gut-punch about what could happen if we don't step up and put a halt to the development. If you're interested, we could turn this into a two-part series, but I understand if you can't spare the column space. And I'll do it for free."

"For free?" Cedric's eyes lit up.

"It's a cause that means a lot to me."

"Well, that's very generous of you. Very generous indeed. Estelle told me you were a man of conscience. I look forward to reading this today. I can get back to you by this evening." Cedric put his hand on Rob's shoulder and walked him into the main office.

"Thank you, Mr Craddock — Cedric. I really appreciate it. You can get me at the number on the cover page."

"If we play our cards right, we can get this into our next edition which Brenda's laying out right now. Brenda!" Cedric snapped.

Startled out of the focused attention she was giving the article she was working on, she looked up. Once again, the errant strand of hair fell across her sweat-dampened face.

"Have Mr Hanson sign a standard contract, and kill the sewing circle article. We have to make space for the

Marsh Island piece," he yelled as he returned to his office and slammed the door.

Rob thought, *If this were an old Hollywood movie, someone would have yelled, "Stop the presses!"*

Brenda just sighed and said to no one in particular, "But I just finished setting the piece…" She slid a paper across the counter to Rob. "Sign and date on the bottom line. It's all the standard stuff. And I heard you say you were doing this for free" — she looked up at him — "thin walls. I hear everything — so if that's the case, strike out this section and initial here."

* * * *

The two visitors made it into the living room and looked at Kevin who stood there in stretched-out track pants and a sweatshirt. Like Mitch, he'd had run-ins with the law and recognised these two for what they were.

"Are you Robert Hanson?" she asked Kevin.

The female was obviously the one in control.

"No. I just used to sleep with him. He's my brother's now. We were taught to share our toys."

"Do you have a name?"

"Kevin Carcross," he answered as he flopped down on the couch.

"Tell me what's happening," Mitch prodded.

Now the male spoke up. "Do you two live here with Mr Hanson?"

"This is my house. I own it."

"Well, that's a point of contention," Kevin interjected.

"Rob and my brother are staying here," Mitch continued. "You still didn't answer my question. Who are you? Or do I have to call the police?"

"No need to, Mr Carcross," the female answered, pulling out a small leather folder from her inside jacket pocket. "We are the police. RCMP. Inspector Sandra Collins, and this is Staff Sergeant Bill Needy. You have nothing to worry about. We're here looking for Robert Hanson. You said that Mr Hanson is not in. Will he be back soon?"

"He went to Victoria for a meeting. He said he should be back by tonight if…nothing holds him up."

Sergeant Needy picked up the questioning. "Mr Carcross—"

"Me or him?" Kevin asked. "I mean we're both Mr Carcross, after all." Mitch stared at his brother. Was he flirting with this guy?

"Him," Needy answered sharply. "You stated that you were Mr Hanson's boyfriend?" he asked Mitch.

"No. I said that," Kevin interjected. "I used to be the boyfriend before he ruined my life."

"I didn't ask you," Needy shot back.

"Are you Mr Hanson's partner?" Inspector Collins asked Mitch, taking control of the questioning.

"We've been seeing each other for about a week now. He was here to write a story about Marsh Island, and we…connected."

"I know more about his past, if that will be of any help in this situation," Kevin added.

"Thank you, Mr… Can we use your first names just to keep things clear?" asked Collins.

"Sure," replied Mitch.

"Works for me. What shall I call you?" Kevin asked Needy.

"Staff Sergeant. Or Sir."

"Now, Mitchell," Collins interjected, "you have no definite time for his return?"

"No, I don't. Like I said before, it'll depend on how his meeting went, and if he made his ferry connections."

"Who was this meeting with and what was it about?" Needy asked.

"I'm not sure," Mitch replied. "He said it was with a publisher in Victoria."

"Do you know what the publication was?" Collins pressed.

"He might have mentioned it, but I don't remember."

Collins referred to her notes. "And you said it was about an article he was writing about this island."

"Yes. He was going to try to help us stop a development that will ruin the mountain."

"So, this had nothing to do with his recent stay in Somalia?" Needy asked pointedly.

"No. Nothing to do with that. He wasn't even sure why that guy wanted money from him."

"Money?" Kevin asked, truly surprised.

"What's this about money?" Needy asked, now taking notes.

"He didn't say."

"And you didn't ask?" Needy inquired.

"I—I don't remember." Mitch's head was spinning.

"Does the name Abdi Mohamed mean anything to you?" Collins asked.

"No. Is that the guy blackmailing Rob?"

"No. It's the nephew of the President of Somalia. The guy your boyfriend's accused of gunning down in cold blood," Needy said.

The blood drained out of Mitch's face.

"No fucking kidding?" Kevin said as a small smile played at the corner of his lips. Mitch slipped slowly into a chair.

"The ferry operator has been notified to call us if Mr Hanson attempts a crossing," Collins informed them. "If he contacts you in the meantime, you'd be wise to call us immediately. We'll be staying at the hotel in town." She handed Mitch her business card.

They left, closing the door behind them.

"Fuck," Kevin said. "Did you get a look at that guy, Needy? I swear if I'd been alone with him, he would have had me in cuffs, pants around my ankles — "

"Stop!" Mitch yelled.

"Too bad about his name. I don't think I could do someone with a name like that."

"Will you shut up?"

"What?"

"Shut…the fuck…up!"

"Hey, I'm just trying to lighten the mood, you know."

"The cops just barged in and accused Rob of being a murderer. I don't think now is the time to lighten the mood."

Mitch went to the refrigerator, took out a bottle of wine and poured himself a large glass.

"I'll have one while you're at it," said Kevin.

"No. You don't have the right to get drunk right now. I get drunk, you revel in what just happened. That's what you do, isn't it? Revel when things in my life go to rat shit because yours is already there."

"Hey. There's no reason to talk to me like that." Kevin stood up. "I'm on your side. I warned you about Rob. I told you to watch out for him. He's just a loser who'll do anything for a buck. This whole thing was probably some big-ass drug deal gone wrong. I've seen it happen."

"No, Rob isn't into drugs," Mitch protested.

"Never said he was using. He'd never wanna get down with the users. Too dirty for mister pretty-boy. He's got more of a supplier vibe."

"I can't believe that."

"Or, Christ, maybe he was over there and thought he could get himself some rich black ass and things went south." Kevin leaned into him. "Probably... probably misread the situation, came onto this Mohamed guy who freaked out all over him and he had to kill him to get away."

Mitch stared at the floor and said, "You really think he could have done it?"

"I've seen him wig out on a guy who called him a fag."

"This is a little different, don't you think?"

"I tell you, he's a predator," Kevin warned him.

"We'll find out what's going on when he gets back," Mitch said, then settled into the couch and waited.

Chapter Fifteen

Rob drove home. He liked the sound of that. *Home. Home is where your Mitch is. Far better than home is where you hang your hat.*

Rob arrived at Francis and Frances' ferry dock in plenty of time for the next crossing. He pulled in behind a large pickup truck. In the bed of the truck was a large steel cage containing an equally large hog. On the cage was a blue ribbon. It seemed that the pig was coming home from a fair where it had won a prize for being...well, for being a big, beautiful pig.

Rob stared at the pig, the pig stared back and it seemed to smile. Rob smiled back. The pig nodded his head up and down. Rob laughed, then nodded back to the pig. *Maybe he's happy at winning first prize.* Rob's conversation with his new porcine friend was interrupted by a startling rap on his window. It was Francis.

Rob had never spoken to the husband before. He was the silent partner in the relationship. She was the face of the operation.

"Mr Hanson," Francis nodded. "That'll be seventy dollars."

"Fares go up?" Rob said, reaching for his wallet.

"Just charge what the wife tells me to," he said, taking the money.

"I've never seen you work the customers before. Is Frances sick today?"

"Not sick. Pissed about somethin', though. Been pissed better part o' the past few days. Best stay away from her if I were you," said the gentle giant, who then sauntered back towards the ferry preparing to board the other passengers.

Rob looked forward. His new pig friend stared at him and slowly began to shake his head from side to side. The pig was no longer smiling. Perhaps he had realised that the blue ribbon was for more than being beautiful and that sometimes a triumphant day meant being one step closer to the dinner table.

Twenty minutes later, Rob pulled up to Mitch's house and leapt out. He was anxious to tell him the news about his meeting with Cedric. He came into the kitchen where Mitch stood alone at the counter staring out the window. Rob could sense the tension.

"You would not believe the trip I've had. I've got great news," Rob said, throwing his arms around Mitch and going in for a kiss. Mitch's shoulders and back were like iron, his lips like stone. "What's wrong? What happened?"

"We had visitors this morning," Mitch said.

"Oh? Who?"

"The RCMP. Were you ever going to tell me you murdered a man or was that not part of your plan?"

"What?" Rob was in shock. He hadn't imagined facing up to this on his return, if ever.

Kevin entered the room. He had changed out of his sloppy clothes into a neat shirt and khakis. He stood to the side and observed.

Mitch's eyes were as cold as ice. "The police seem to think you're involved in the murder of some guy named Abdi Mohamed."

"My God, that was Abdi? I had no idea. Things happened so quickly."

"So, you admit it? You killed a man!" Mitch yelled.

Rob tried to stay calm. "No...I was just there when it happened. It was an accident. I swear it."

"It was an accident that you were there when the nephew of the President of Somalia was murdered?"

The telephone in the kitchen began to ring.

"No. Abdi was my driver," Rob continued, "not the President's nephew. He wasn't even a great driver. He robbed me and I chased after him."

"Is that why you killed him? Because he robbed you?"

Irritated by the ringing phone, Kevin answered it. "Hello? ...Yeah, he's here. Who's calling? ...Okay. Hang on."

"No," Rob tried to explain. "He just ran into a gun battle in the street as I chased him."

"Hey, Robby, there's a call for you. Some guy named Cedric Craddock."

"It's my publisher. Tell him I'll get back to him."

"Wait a minute. Cedric Craddock. You're working for Craddock?" Mitch demanded.

"Yeah."

"Cedric Craddock is the head of Peak Capital Developments."

"No. This Cedric Craddock is a magazine publisher."

"On Broughton Street in Victoria?"

"Yeah."

"I can't believe it. I can't believe you're working for him of all people. Craddock is the one in charge of the development that's going to ruin the island. Was it the money? Is that what made you do it?"

"No, I was doing it for my agent, and then when I met you, I was going to do it to help you."

"What kind of sick mind would think that having my home bulldozed into the ground was helping?"

"I don't know what's happening. Please believe me, I haven't done anything wrong."

"I can accept the fact that you've lied to me, and used me—"

"He also tried to fuck that Eric guy, didn't he?" Kevin added.

"But I cannot accept," Mitch continued, "what you've done to my home and family. Now, get out! It's over."

Mitch ran off to the bedroom and slammed the door.

"Rob's busy at the moment," Kevin muttered into the phone. "I'll have him call you back. Bye bye!" He hung up.

Just then there was a knock at the door. Neither Kevin nor Rob moved to answer.

"You never change, do you Robby?" Kevin sneered.

A second set of knocks, this time more insistent, sent Rob to the door. Two RCMP personnel stood at the entrance.

"Robert Hanson?"

"Yes."

"I'm Inspector Sandra Collins and this is Staff Sergeant Bill Needy. RCMP."

"Oh," said Rob, feeling even more defeated than before.

"This just keeps getting better," Kevin gloated.

"Mr Hanson, were you aware that we were looking for you?"

"I…I'm sorry, things have been a bit crazy…but…"

"Were you not told that Staff Sergeant Needy and I had been by earlier and had requested that we be contacted as soon as you returned?"

Rob looked at Kevin, who shrugged. "I guess I forgot."

"Well, thankfully the ferry operator was more cooperative."

"Look, I just came through the door."

"Would you please get your coat and car keys, Mr Hanson?"

"Why? Where are we going?"

"Victoria. Beyond that, well, that depends on how cooperative you are."

"Better and better." This time Kevin laughed. He sauntered back into the room and handed Rob his belongings. Mitch had crammed everything into a carryall and left it outside the bedroom door.

* * * *

The trip to Victoria was quiet. Collins rode with Rob, and Needy followed. Francis made a special crossing just for them. Frances was there but, other than glowering at Rob, she communicated nothing.

At the RCMP office, Rob waited three hours for Chief Inspector Chris Mali who oversaw the meeting. Much to Rob's relief, it was more of a questioning than interrogation and the wait had allowed Rob time to review the pertinent events in Somalia that had led to all of this.

The meeting was recorded and, having given up the option of having legal representation present, Rob told his version of the events of the night which ended with the shooting of his driver.

"And that covers everything, Mr Hanson?" Mali asked.

"Everything as I remember it."

Mali referred to his notes. "And this man Yussuf..."

"Yussuf. Yussuf Ali."

"This Mr Ali—do you have any way of contacting him?"

"Yes..." Rob started to root through his carryall, finally finding his notebook. "It'll...be here... Here it is!" He slid the book over to the Chief Inspector, pointing to the name and his cell number. Rob was always amazed that, no matter the level of apparent poverty and hardship, people in the farthest-flung reaches of the earth had cell phones.

"And you met this man how?" Mali continued.

"Through a UN contact of mine. He recommended him as my guide for this trip."

"Okay. I'll pass it on to Monsieur Robichaud in Dubai and he'll follow up on it. So, will you be any easier to find on Marsh Island if we have any further questions?"

"Actually...I won't be heading back there," Rob replied. "I was hoping to return to Toronto if I'm allowed to. I think you know my address there."

"It's on file. At this point there's nothing to hold you here. Check in with our local office when you get home."

"Thank you, sir."

And with that, Rob left the office.

* * * *

Rob remembered very little of the journey from the police station to Vancouver. The ferry ride from Swartz Bay to Tsawwassen on the mainland was an endless trip of emptiness. He remembered the happiness of the young couple he'd met on the way out, the unspoken fear that he would never find such happiness, and the bliss he had experienced with Mitch. He stared at the waters below and longed for the strength to throw himself into them, vanquishing the pain of his shattered heart.

In Vancouver, he crashed at his sister's. The evening was a wine-soaked blur. He couldn't face a night alone in a hotel, even if it was the Sylvia. He dreaded the thought of going home where he would be alone, haunted by ghosts, of images of Mitch in tears, of Kevin smirking at his humiliation and the fear of the damage Kevin would do to his brother for daring to date his ex.

What if he'd taken his sister up on her offer to set him up with Thom? He seemed like a nice-enough guy and wasn't bad looking. He had a good job. He could have established a nice, solid life here on the west coast. Not a precarious one with a bowl-carving hippy on an unknown island. Well, it wouldn't be unknown for long.

Once his article came out, it would draw attention to the development. But would it come out? Would Cedric still publish it? And why would he publish it if he was behind the development? Rob's mind questioned everything that had happened over the past weeks until his brain gave him up to sleep.

His sister knew well enough not to ask him any questions during his stay. As she dropped him at the airport, she said, "Take good care of yourself. You know I love you." Rob knew she used those words sparingly.

"I love you, too."

With that, he entered the terminal, and in a few hours was flying home.

Chapter Sixteen

Rob opened the door of his house and once inside, leaned against the door to keep out the demons that followed him.

The air was stale. Karen had moved out as soon as the RCMP had started to make inquiries. He would deal with that problem in the morning, but for now, what was that smell? He took a deep breath. Then, like it was a childhood sense memory, he knew. It came from the sweater he wore. He'd left it out on his bed before heading out for his meeting with Cedric. From a time when he was still happy. The sweater smelled of Rufus.

He held it up to his face and breathed in. Then, for the first time, he cried. He cried as he had cried when his parents had died. He'd forgotten how he'd wept back then. A deep, soul-wrenching wail that grew from a life-altering experience. From the death of a part of himself.

The next morning, he woke. He looked out the window which faced the lake. He felt nothing but exhaustion. He'd cried himself out. He was spent, feeling an overwhelming emptiness punctuated with a pain in the pit of his stomach. He had to move on. He knew that much. He'd been through trauma before. He'd handled it then and he could handle it now.

He stepped out of the shower. As he towelled himself dry, he glanced at himself in the mirror. He had aged since he'd last had a good look at himself. He stooped a little, and his stomach sagged. He watched himself closely as he would once have stared at a wild animal in the woods. His breath was shallow, his skin duller than it once had been. It was like looking into the future. One without Mitch.

He stood on the deck staring out at the water. The lake was still. There were no sailboats tacking against the wind. The sky was a lifeless grey. Even nature offered no solace.

Well, he had a book to write. That would fill his time. Writing was a solo sport, and solo was what he did best, wasn't it? He had a lifetime of practice. And he'd promised Estelle he'd get her a draft in the next few months. He'd wasted good time on that puff piece on Marsh Island when he should have been working on the bigger commitment. He should go next door and thank Gina for looking in on the place after Karen left, and maybe he would go out for dinner with Karen. She could always make him laugh. He'd give her a call. But first, he had to go see Estelle and set everything straight with her.

Rob went to the bedroom closet, pulled out a clean pair of jeans and a pressed cotton shirt and got dressed. He made his way to the kitchen. Breakfast was a bowl of yogurt with fruit and a latte. He dropped a blueberry on the floor and for a moment expected Rufus to snuffle by and pick it up. He and Mitch had joked that he was their Roomba. But that was in his previous life. He picked up the blueberry and threw it into the compost bin. He brushed his teeth, grabbed his car keys and headed out to catch a water taxi.

Rob retrieved his car from the spot he rented in a Toronto condo building near the water taxi pier. He liked to drive. Even in the city. He started every trip with a deep breath and a moment of meditative thought — his version of a prayer asking for the strength to detach himself from his emotions so he wouldn't lose it when some asshole driver cut him off or deked into a parking space ahead of him. He would be the Buddha of drivers.

Estelle's office was on a stretch of King Street East populated by design showrooms, law offices and trendy independent coffee houses. He frequented Café Olé when he was in the neighbourhood. Max, the proprietor, greeted him with a smile.

"Rob. Long time no see, man. Been outta town again?"

Rob smiled back. "When am I not out of town?"

"Someplace exotic, I hope. I live through you, you know."

"You'll go somewhere. I know it."

"Not as long as I've got this place to take care of." Max shrugged. "I tell you, it's worse than havin' a kid. Trust me. I know."

"How many is it? Five?"

"Six, my friend. I gotta get this thing tied off," Max said, pointing to his crotch, "or take up with guys like you. You got no idea how lucky you gay guys got it."

"Oh, sometimes it's not all it's cracked up to be."

"Yeah, I guess. So, same order as usual for you and the ladies?" Max asked.

"You got it."

Rob left with a latte for himself and small French roast drip coffees for Estelle and Rosie, then he crossed the street to the office.

* * * *

Fillion Literary Management was on the second floor of a former funeral business established in 1872. The name 'Hallowell's Funeral Parlour' was still engraved in the red sandstone above the front entrance. A men's tailor shop occupied the first floor. Estelle joked that it was a fitting building for two dying professions.

Rob found Rosie in her usual place behind the reception desk. She had been with Estelle for longer than he had, an odd thing for a receptionist in this business. Most tired quickly of the temperaments of the clients or the agents, or both, and moved on to less-demanding employers like doctors' offices or police departments. Rosie was also unusual in that she was a writer. She had initially approached Estelle as a potential client, having written a lust-filled romance called *Summer in the Grass*. Estelle managed to land her both a book and movie deal, then offered Rosie a job as a receptionist. The previous receptionist had left as a result of the tyrannical ranting of Estelle's premier author Michael Frost, who that year had been short-listed for, but not won, the Booker Prize. Estelle encouraged Rosie to continue with her writing career while under her employ. She accepted the offer with the understanding that she did not file or fetch coffee.

"Well, Mr Hanson, it's good to see you again," Rosie said.

"Thanks, Rosie. For you." He handed her the coffee.

"You're sweet. Thank you."

"Is she in?" Rob asked.

"In and waiting for you."

Rob entered Estelle's office. He found her sitting at her desk, behind a pile of manuscripts.

"Robert, darling, how are you?" Estelle growled.

"I've been better."

"I heard that you had a good meeting with Cedric. He loved your article."

"He did?"

"Why wouldn't he?"

"Because it's just what he didn't want!" Rob said, surprised.

Estelle said, "I read it. It was perfect. Beautiful island. Charming inhabitants. Nature, quaint charm. It has a big goofy dog, for Christ's sake. What else would he want?"

"What…did he send you a copy?"

"Yeah. He emailed me a PDF this morning. Here." She passed him a printout.

"What is that guy up to?" Rob scanned the pages. "That bastard!" The blood rushed to his face.

Estelle looked at Rob, puzzled. "What?"

"He cut out everything about the development."

"What development?"

"Can he do that?" Rob asked. "No one's done that before. Can they just go and do that?"

Estelle shook her head. "I told you I didn't handle your contract. What did it say when you read it?"

"I…didn't read the contract," Rob admitted.

"You what?"

"Things were a bit crazy. I didn't even think about it."

Estelle leaned across her desk. "Did he pay you?"

"I…offered it to him for free."

Estelle glowered at Rob, turned to her computer and started typing.

"Well, I was going to get free publicity for the Stop the Development movement," Rob explained.

Estelle finished typing. "I just asked Cedric's assistant for a copy of the contract for my files. You were mentioning development. What the hell is that about?"

"They're going to build a huge development on the island. Hotel, spa, restaurants. Everything! The article I wrote pointed out the hundred ways that would be bad for everyone."

"Well, the article I read will just make people want to come to the island," Estelle shot back.

"Mitch already thinks I did this all on purpose. Now he'll be sure I was working for Cedric. He'll kill me."

Just then Estelle's computer pinged with an incoming email. She opened it and studied the screen.

"The contract clearly stipulates that the article can be edited for size at the editor's discretion. This is bad, Robert. You know you shouldn't have signed this. You handed over complete control to him."

"So, there's nothing we can do?"

"I'll call Cedric and see what I can do, although it might be too late."

"Mitch'll never forgive me."

Rob looked her in the face. Estelle's eyes softened.

"This Mitch, he means a lot to you?"

"I've never felt this way about anyone."

Estelle got up from behind her desk and walked her five-foot frame over until she stood right in front of him.

"You've got it bad," she said.

"Oh, that's putting it mildly."

"Does he feel the same way?"

"He did, until he thought I had a thing for his neighbour. And then there was the murder charge and now this."

"Robert, in my world that just makes you interesting. Now, this murder thing…?"

"It's nothing. I think I got it all cleared it up with the RCMP, but this" — he waved the printout of the article — "he'll never forgive me." His voice cracked. Estelle opened her arms wide, looking at him in a motherly way. He moved in for a hug, and she slapped him full force across the face. The shock did its job.

"Now you listen up. When you were on the side of that mountain and your rope snapped, did you just let yourself fall?"

"You hit me!" he whimpered, out of shock more than pain.

"Did you fall?" she yelled.

"No!"

"What did you do?"

"I grabbed onto a rock."

"That's right. You fought back. You didn't give in. You never give in. That's what's sold you nearly fifty thousand books. You're a fighter, Robert, and that's what people like. That's why you're a success. This," she said, indicating the slouched figure in front of her, "this isn't a success. You wanna behave like this, you switch to writing romance novels."

"Well…"

"So, now that you've managed to beat a murder rap—"

"I didn't beat it. I didn't kill anyone."

"Are you going to keep interrupting me?"

"No."

"Good. As I was saying—now that you've managed to beat a murder rap, are you going to lay down and play dead, or are you going to fight to save this thing you have with this Mitch guy?"

"I'm not sure how—" Rob stopped talking as he saw Estelle winding up for another slap.

"Stop thinking," she said, "and start doing. Obviously thinking is not your strong suit. Now, come here." Estelle opened her arms wide once more. Rob came in for a hug and she slapped him again.

"What was that for?" he yelled, his cheek burning.

"That was for signing a contract without reading it."

* * * *

"You need to get right out there and get laid." Karen was serious. "Come on. Get outta those sloppy shorts and throw on something tight. I mean, really tight, cuz I'm taking you out to the Nail Bar. My treat."

The Nail Bar? Things happened to people who went there. He should just stick to dinner tonight... But why? Wasn't he a single guy now? Single, not bad looking and loaded? Hell—the Nail Bar was probably the one place he should go tonight.

The Nail Bar was one of Toronto's cruisiest pickup joints, set up behind a nail salon on Church Street. It was rumoured that even a corpse could get lucky at the Nail. He wasn't sure if he should take the invitation as a compliment or a comment on his run-down condition.

They arrived at eleven. The place was just starting to pick up. Karen made a big deal of buying the first round of drinks. Rob had to smile. She was still using his credit card.

Karen spotted a tall, muscular blond across the bar. "Ooh, look at that one. You should ask Thor to dance."

"Why, when I've got you?"

They downed their drinks, then a second round like a couple of teenagers, then Rob grabbed Karen by the hand and headed onto the dance floor.

While he had no definable dance form, Rob moved with a sensuality that was a magnet to any gay man's eyes. Two songs into the set, the tall blond moved onto the dance floor and began to orbit around him. Karen slowly drifted back as Thor began to descend for a landing on Planet Rob. He just kept bopping to the music, his mind freed for the moment from everything that had happened over the past few days.

By the third song, Thor had manoeuvred his way behind Rob, inches away from his back. He slid his hands under Rob's arms, which were raised above his head, and wrapped them around his muscled chest, hands massaging his nipples. Without missing a beat, Rob rotated and they moved together chest to chest for a moment before lips locked and tongues entwined. Rob didn't even notice that Karen had worked her way through the crowded dance floor and out onto the street.

The night ended up at Rob's. Clothes were tossed by the front door. Words were not spoken. Mouths joined, tongues massaged orifices, probing deeply, making way for other body parts. Bestial groans and moans filled the air. Chests heaved, hips thrust, hair matted with sweat, and bodies were soaked with fluid.

They showered together, kissing passionately, then gently. They dried off. Thanks were given. No names were exchanged. The blond left and Rob got ready for bed. He never thought to see if the guy could even find the water taxi stand.

He sat there on the edge of his bed. He should have felt satisfied, like he'd just had a great work out, but he didn't. What he felt was empty. Emptiness tinged with guilt. It made no sense. Hadn't Mitch thrown him out of his life? *I'm not cheating on anyone. I could fuck a hundred guys, like...whoever that was. I owe nothing to anyone.*

He spotted his camera on the dresser. He had dropped it there when he got home. *Fuck him. If he doesn't want me in his life, I won't have him in mine,* he thought, and he grabbed the camera, and powered it up in order to delete the images. But instead of deleting them en masse, he found himself scrolling through the record of his journey. The shots of the kid on the ferry — *I should send him the pics of him and his boyfriend* — the light-dappled road leading to the cemetery, the church — *I'll hold on to those. I might be able to use them somewhere or sell the rights to them at least. They were good shots* — and Mitch. Frame after frame of that beautiful man. His gorgeous broad smile, those bottomless blue eyes. Rob's heart shattered all over again. And there was that feeling deep inside the pit of his stomach that left him short of breath. He couldn't give up and pretend he could just walk away like nothing had happened. He had to fix this. He had to find a way to make it better.

* * * *

Mitch walked into the kitchen. He hadn't shaved in over a week. He had passed beyond the sexy scruffy look into dishevelled. He'd worn the same clothes for several days — grubby jeans and a stretched-out t-shirt.

"Have you seen Rufus?" he asked his brother. They were the first words he had spoken in two days.

"Nope," Kevin answered, then went back to drinking his beer.

Mitch went back outside and called the dog's name. "Where are you?" He hadn't seen him since Rob had left. It wasn't like the dog not to be there when he needed him. Rufus had the ability to know when there was a problem.

Mitch started walking. He had no destination in mind, but his feet knew where he had to go. They headed him in the direction of the Peak. It was a walk of several hours, and all the time, he kept his eyes peeled. The forest was silent. Too silent.

"Rufus. Here, boy."

He crossed the road that led to Admiral's Peak. He had been walking for hours on little sleep or food. Mitch was exhausted. He felt his world spiralling out of control. It seemed that everything he found comfort in was slipping away.

He sat down in the shade of a tall arbutus tree. His eyes drifted off into the distance as he watched a large turkey vulture circling the sky. He wished he could be that bird, way up high above all the cares of humanity, just living for the sake of living. Nothing more. *Why do people make life so complicated? Animals have it right,* he thought as his eyes slowly closed and he drifted off to sleep.

* * * *

The party was loud and out of control. His twenty-year-old mind revelled in the chaos. The acid had kicked in some time ago — how long ago he didn't know. Time lost all meaning. Nothing had meaning and everything had meaning all at the same time. What had been Mitchell Carcross ceased to exist. That man's problems were someone else's. This Mitchell was free from all cares.

Colours ran. Shapes ran. Bodies morphed into one. There was no thought. No judgement. At one moment he was deeply focused on running his fingers through a girl's hair, marvelling at the details of each strand. His eyes were microscopes and he focused on the individual scales of each strand. The next moment his lips fused with the lips of another. Was it a man? Who knew? Who cared? He sensed he was safe in this stranger's lips, soft and sensuous. He felt their tongues merge, their cells intermingle, their atoms pass through each other. They were truly one. Then a voice...familiar?

"You're still tense," he said. The voice was a man's. His features started to come into focus, then blurred into atoms. "You'll feel so much better if you relax. It's the only way."

The first's lips kissed him again. His tongue penetrated him and he became a cell dividing in two, and two into four. He was multiplying.

"Here," said the familiar voice. "This will help. Give me your arm. This won't hurt. Just a small prick."

And he felt the warmth spread throughout his body, wrapping its arms around him like a hug, lulling him to sleep.

The man with the voice held his arm firmly. A strong man. He could feel his confidence in his every move. For the first time, Mitch stared him in the face. It was Kevin. He felt himself starting to lose consciousness. The last thing he remembered was his brother's voice saying, "There. You'll be okay now, Mitchy. I'll take care of you." Then, to someone else, "Give him a few minutes, then do what you want. It's a hundred bucks." Then Mitch felt himself being turned over and he greeted the blackness.

Chapter Seventeen

Ricky Daniels drove his truck up to the ferry dock on Gabriola Island. He had his instructions. *"If the woman doesn't let you on the ferry, hand her this letter."* He patted the vest pocket and reassured himself that the letter was still there. *Why can't people just let me do my job? Why do they have to make things so complicated?*

He pulled his truck forward and a large woman approached. He found her appearance, in both bulk and scowl, intimidating as hell. Ricky was twenty years old with a tidy five-and-a-half-foot frame and weighed in at one hundred and forty pounds soaking wet. He was the newbie on the crew.

"Where you goin'?" she barked.

"Marsh Island. Where else do you go? Catalina?" Frank Peterson, the crew chief, piped up from the front passenger seat. Frank was equal to the woman in girth and scowl and was not in the mood for any bullshit. He'd been up since five and had terrible constipation, something he got any time he had to travel for work anywhere off Vancouver Island.

"What's yer purpose on the island?"

"Some people are doing some work on their property and we're just going to do some survey work," Ricky said.

"Survey work, huh?"

"Yeah."

"Doesn't have anythin' to do with Admiral's Peak, does it?"

"Well," Ricky started.

"What business is it of yours what we're going to do over there?" Frank snarled back. "We don't have time to play around. Give her the letter," he snapped at Ricky.

Ricky fumbled at his vest pocket and pulled out the letter which he passed with shaky hands to Frances.

"This is an official letter from the government giving us permission to conduct our business on the island," he stuttered out, adding, "Ma'am," in the hopes it would help. He had no idea why they would need a letter from the government to get access to the island, or why anyone would care if they were there. They were only a survey crew, after all.

Frances took the letter and opened it. She then fussed, making a scene out of getting her glasses out of her overall pocket and sitting them on her face. Once in position she looked at Ricky, hoping he saw what an inconvenience he'd caused her. She glanced at the letter. It was on what appeared to be official government letterhead and dated the day before.

Francis approached the truck.

"Problem, Frances?" he asked.

"You tell me, Francis," she replied, then read the letter out loud.

"Dear Mr and Mrs McKinnon,

"I hope this letter finds you well, and business brisk.

"I am writing to ensure that you offer this survey crew every possible assistance in their effort to gain access to Marsh Island. I would hate to think you might do anything to impede their efforts. The government does not want another incident such as that which befell the cellular telephone operations installers. One wouldn't want such an incident to have a negative effect on your operations licence which, I believe, is coming up for renewal next spring.

"Sincerely,

"Hugh McCutcheon

"MLA for Salish-North Islands."

Frances carefully removed her glasses and looked at her husband.

Francis looked concerned then indicated to her that she should let them board. She handed Ricky back the letter. Ricky had shifted the transmission into drive when Frances said, "Hundred an' five dollars."

"What?" Ricky replied.

"Hundred an' five dollars for passage."

"Oh," he said, reaching for his wallet.

"Cash," she said, pointing to a small, hand-written sign that read *No credit or debit cards.*

"Cash?" Ricky looked at Frank. "I just have credit cards." The other three men in the truck searched their wallets but only came up with seventy-six dollars among them.

"There's a cash machine up at the bank back up the hill and to the right. We leave in fifteen minutes with or without you. Nothin' stands in the way of the schedule. Not even McCutcheon."

They made it with three minutes to spare. Ricky Daniels was a wreck. This was his first day on the job, first time out of a big city and first time in the wilderness. He'd survived the first test, but he wondered what more dangerous challenges he might come across.

* * * *

Kevin had just woken from a nap and was looking in the fridge for something to eat.

"Nothing but yogurt and vegetables. How the hell does Mitch stay alive?" he muttered to himself. He heard footsteps on gravel. They moved quickly. Feet hammered up the front porch steps. The front door opened as though it had been kicked in. His brother stood in the entrance, his face red with rage and streaked with tears. He was panting as if he had run a long distance in a short time.

"Why did you do it?" Mitch yelled.

"What the hell's up with you? You look like shit."

Mitch charged at him like a wild animal. For the first time, Kevin was terrified by his kid brother. He'd never seen him act this way. He swung around the kitchen island, keeping it between them.

"Why did you do it?" Mitch was weeping. "Why did you ruin my life?"

"Ruin your... What are you talking about? Are you on something?" Kevin yelled.

"You should know."

"I should know what?" Kevin snarled.

"What the hell I'm on. You were the one who shot me up with it!"

Mitch stared Kevin down.

"Look here, Mitchy, I can see something's wrong. You want me to call your doctor?"

Mitch dodged around the island to catch him, but Kevin stayed one step ahead.

"I remember it all now. It's all come back," Mitch said. "You fucking shot me up with heroin, didn't you? You did it again and again and again."

"No, little brother. You got that wrong."

"You got me hooked on that shit and ruined my fucking life!"

With near superhuman strength, Mitch vaulted over the island and tackled his brother, pinning him to the ground.

"You fucking…took…away…my…life!" he yelled, punctuating each word by driving Kevin's head into the floor.

"Stop it! Stop it, please!" Kevin cried. "I didn't do it. You were spinning out of control all by yourself. Don't you remember?"

"I remember everything now."

"I don't think you know what you remember. Your brain's all messed up, man. You fried your brain all by yourself."

"You sold me to other guys while I was fried!" Mitch shouted.

"What the fuck are talking about?"

"You let other guys fuck me. You sold me to other guys. To fuck! Why!?"

"It was probably some other guy you hooked up with. It wasn't me. I swear it," Kevin pleaded.

Mitch grabbed Kevin by his shoulders and shook him. "Stop lying to me!"

"I'm not lying. Trust me. I'm your brother. Why would I want to hurt you? I've spent my life looking out for you."

"You've spent your life taking advantage of me."

"That's bullshit and you know it," Kevin barked.

"Bullshit? Like you telling everyone that this is your house?"

"Well, it should have been," Kevin countered. "She had no right to cut me out of her will like that. I had every right to this house. You didn't. I'm the oldest! I was there for that old broad when she needed work done around the place while you were off at school partying your face off."

"And you hated me for it, didn't you? You were stuck here working when no one else would hire you."

Kevin pushed Mitch away. "And who's fault was that? That money-grubbing boyfriend of yours. If you're looking for someone who ruins lives, it's him. He wrecked any chances I ever had, just because he couldn't keep his pecker in his pants. He only wanted you because of that ass of yours and the money you have in this place. How long do you think he would have stuck around with all your pathetic whining about how hard done by you were, especially with that paycheque the developer waved in his face? How long?"

"So, I made a mistake with him, but at least he didn't try to kill me."

"Stop blaming everybody else for your own bad choices," Kevin yelled.

Mitch slapped Kevin hard across the face as he straddled his chest.

"Didn't I warn you about him? Didn't I tell you what he was like?" Kevin cried.

Mitch stood up and raised his foot. He positioned his boot heel above his brother's head. Kevin closed his eyes in terror and began to whimper. His body began to shake. His bladder emptied itself. He waited for the final blow…but nothing happened. Kevin opened his eyes and saw Mitch slowly lower his boot to the floor beside Kevin's head.

Kevin shimmied back out of striking distance, leaving a slug-like trail of urine behind him. He was able to get to his feet. He tried to speak but his fear and anger garbled the thoughts and words.

"Get the fuck out of my house," Mitch commanded in a frighteningly calm voice. "Pack up your shit and get out and never come back again."

"But, Mitchy…I'm your brother. You've got no one else."

"I'm better off on my own."

Ten minutes later Kevin emerged from the guest room with his duffle bag. Kevin felt the truth of the situation set in. He had always needed Mitch more than Mitch had needed him.

"Please…"

Mitch said nothing.

Kevin walked to the front door as a man walked to the noose.

"You want to know why I did that to you?"

Mitch just stared, his eyes lifeless.

Kevin turned and with one final attack. "You had everything back then, and what did I have? Nothing!" he spit out. "You're gonna find out fast that sometimes you gotta sell whatever you got if you're gonna survive out there. And for me, Mitchy, that was you."

Kevin left the house, slamming the door behind him.

Chapter Eighteen

It was the day after Rob met with Estelle, and his face still stung from her slaps to his face, but sometimes that was just what a guy needed. Not that Rob was into that sort of thing. Pain wasn't for enjoyment, but it was an inducement to deal with an issue — when a person's tooth throbs, they go and see a dentist, when their ankle screams in pain, they stop moving until they can extract their foot from the crevice, when their chest hurts, they get to the hospital before the heart attack kills them. Estelle's slaps had told him to stop feeling sorry for himself and act. If Mitch meant something to him, which he did, then Rob had to figure out how to undo the damage and get him back.

When it came to solving problems, Rob was methodical. Step one — identify the problem he faced. Step two — identify his assets. Step three — identify which assets would best be suited to fighting the problem.

The problem at hand — prove to Mitch that he wasn't a murderer and that he wasn't a willing participant in the pending destruction of his home and life.

His assets — good looks, intelligence, good friends and a persuasive writing skill that had garnered him a strong social media following. The first might work if he were dealing with a shallow, self-centred man. The last three, however...he had an idea of where to begin.

He readjusted his schedule for the next few weeks and called Karen.

"Hey. It's me."

"Well, you sound chipper. Can I assume that you had a fun time with Geoffrey?"

"Who's Geoffrey?" he asked.

"The guy you hooked up with last night? God — you guys are useless. When you take someone back to your place, you've at least gotta get their name, if not name and number. What if something went missing and you'd had to call the cops?"

Rob thought for a moment. "How did you know he came back to my place?"

"Well, first off, he's a Greek god."

"Last night you called him Thor. Thor was a Norse god," Rob corrected.

"Norse, Greek, what's the difference? He was as hot as they come. Secondly, I haven't heard you this perky in ages."

"I am not perky. Perky is for puppies and cheerleaders."

"Oh, you're perky all right. And thirdly," she continued, "I bumped into Reggie, the bouncer at the Nail, and he told me you two left together, which means you either went back to his place, a small studio on Isabella Street which he shares with his sister, lucky bitch, or yours. And if I were the one trying to impress a Norse god, your place wins hands down. And before you ask, Reggie told me where Geoffrey lived. Did you cook him up a nice breakfast? A boy like that needs plenty of protein."

"Well, we had a nice time. He didn't stay over."

"What! Why?" she shot back.

"It was a fun time and let's leave it at that."

"But I wanted you two to hit it off so I could show him off. Sometimes you are so selfish."

He knew she was just kidding, partially.

"Look, let me make it up to you," Rob consoled. "Lunch at that Yorkville restaurant you've been talking about. We'll go and out-snoot the snooty staff and make them hate us even more when we tip them well."

"What are you up to?"

"Can't I take my best friend out for lunch without an ulterior motive?"

"No. But I'll let you get away with it this time."

He smiled. "Good. I'll pick you up at noon. Oh, and pack some things. You can crash at my place for a few weeks. And don't worry about the cops. I think everything's all cleared up."

"Where to this time?"

"I'll tell you at lunch."

The next day, Rob was on Air Canada Flight 195 bound for Victoria.

* * * *

Rob arrived at the Broughton Street offices of Vancouver Island Publishing at 10:25 when he knew Cedric Craddock would have just arrived but would still be in a good mood before the cares of the day wore him thin.

Rob entered the main office to find it unstaffed. Brenda was not at her spot. Her coffee cup by her keyboard was still full. Perhaps she had stepped out to the washroom. Undaunted, Rob headed towards the inner office door, which he found ajar. He could hear Cedric on the telephone.

"What kind of idiot puts that sort of thing in writing? Do you have any idea what would happen if those fools on the island got a hold of something like this? And on Ministry letterhead?…Honestly, McCutcheon, if you hadn't picked up the bar tabs for half of your constituents, I don't think you would ever have been elected. We'll talk about this later."

He hung up. Rob knocked and entered. Cedric quickly put down a piece of paper, which Rob presumed was the subject of the phone call, and shifted a file folder to cover it.

"Mr Hanson? What are you — did Brenda show you in?"

"No. There was no one at the desk so I took the chance that you might be in."

"I thought you'd be back in Toronto by now."

"No. Still around," Rob said.

Cedric smiled. "So, what can I do for you?"

"I was curious about my article for *West Coast Travel*."

"Oh. What about it?"

"Well, first off, the photo of the image of Gabriola Island from the ferry should have been credited to Kyle Marshall, not me."

"Oh dear," Cedric replied, "we can't have that happen. We have a reputation for accuracy that is unparalleled."

"I'm glad to hear that."

"That would have been a mix-up on Brenda's part. I'll have her correct the online version immediately. She'll contact Mister…"

"Marshall," Rob offered.

"Mr Marshall, and extend our deepest apologies explaining the error and what we can, and can't do about it at this stage."

"I'm glad to hear that. Look, I don't want to step on any toes, but if I may make a suggestion?"

"Which is…" Cedric said with some hesitation in his voice.

"Kyle is an excellent photographer."

"The photo was a good shot, as I recall."

"He just needs experience," Rob explained. "Perhaps you could contract him for a local shoot when the opportunity arises. He's a natural and, with his lack of professional credits, you could get him for a song. It's a win-win situation."

"Well, I'll give that some consideration." Cedric said.

Rob said, "Do you mind if I sit down?"

"No, not at all," Cedric replied.

Rob continued, "Now, as for my other challenge. You seem to have edited the piece in such a way as to change the whole point of it."

"The point of the article was to be a puff piece on an unknown island in two thousand words. What you provided me with was a well-written political diatribe of thirty-five hundred words. I simply edited it for size.

For the story to maintain any coherence, I had no choice but to lose the eco-politics."

"But—"

"Mr Hanson, there are no buts in the publishing business. If we don't give the readers what they want, they will not buy, and what they want is to be inspired, not made to feel guilty."

"But don't you have a responsibility to the writer?"

"I counter with this—doesn't the writer have a responsibility to read their contract?"

With this Cedric turned and opened his filing cabinet drawer. "Marsh Island," he continued to preach as he searched through his files, "is now old news to my readers. They are consumers who gobble up lightweight fluff disguised as learned prose. The sooner you realise that the pap you write is the junk food of the literary world, the better. It's consumed one moment and shit out the next, soon to be forgotten as they move on to something new."

In the few moments it took Cedric to locate and extract the contract, Rob reached over and stole the letter Cedric had been trying to hide.

"As you can see, Mr Hanson," Cedric said, handing Rob his contract, "you have agreed to have the piece edited for length...at the editor's discretion...as you would have known had you read your contract. Something I am sure your agent would have recommended. And to show how much I appreciate your talents, I will pay you in full in spite of your kind offer to give it to us for free. I'll write you a cheque right now." As Cedric rooted through the chaos of his desk, looking for his cheque book, which he extracted from a pile of papers, he continued to speak as he hastily scribbled in the details on a blank cheque. "Now, any attempt to sabotage the development at this point is too little, too late. The cogs are already turning quickly on that project." He tore the cheque from the book and handed it to Rob. "There. Now, be a good boy, take the money and get the fuck out of my office."

There was nothing he could come up with to fight the facts. But that wasn't why he'd paid Cedric a visit.

Rob left the office and noticed Brenda was still not at her post. Either she'd eaten something that didn't agree with her or she'd gotten fed up working for that asshole and abandoned ship. When Rob reached the street, he pulled his phone from his pocket and switched off the record feature, then glanced at the paper he'd liberated from Cedric's desk. Rob smiled. He'd come to Cedric's office with the feeble hope that he would catch him saying something more incriminating than an insulting remark about the intelligence of his readership. He'd walked out with something far better. He put the letter back into his jacket pocket. The satisfying crackle of folded paper reassured him that he still had a fighting chance.

Rob reached his hotel room, opened his computer and began to write.

A time comes to each and every one of us when we are called upon to take a stance against an injustice, when we are asked to take up arms against a tyranny which threatens the soul of what we hold dear to us.

This was to be his manifesto to save Marsh Island and to prove himself to the man he had fallen in love with.

Chapter Nineteen

Ricky turned up the dirt and gravel road.

"Are you sure this is where we're supposed to go?"

Frank looked at him. "What did I ever do to deserve you? Oh yeah, you're the boss' son."

Ricky wasn't used to off-road driving. Country roads like the one to Tofino were rough enough for him.

"It's not even really a road," Ricky muttered.

"Will you just drive?" Frank sighed. The other two in the back said nothing.

"But what if we get stuck? Look!" he said, holding his cell phone up to Frank's face. "No bars!"

"Give me that," he said, snatching the phone from his hands. "Watch where you're going," he yelled as Ricky almost missed a sharp hairpin curve in the road.

"S-sorry. I'm just not good with being out here."

"Pull over."

"No, I'll be all right."

"Pull the truck over! That curve's not on the map."

Ricky pulled over to what might be called the shoulder. The men got out and Frank laid out the topographic map of the island on the hood of the truck. They huddled around as he traced the route from the ferry landing. Ricky stood by nervously keeping his eyes open for danger. A turkey vulture circled above.

"What's that?" he said.

"Just a vulture. Probably scoutin' out dead things t' eat," offered Marco, the team's driller.

"What do they eat?" Ricky asked nervously.

"Carrion." Seeing the blank look in Ricky's eyes, Marco explained, "Dead things...like scraps left over from a wolf kill."

"Wolf?" Ricky was terrified by even the thought of wolves, having been brought up on a diet of fairy tales and horror films. In his mind the wolf was the pinnacle of evil—the cruellest, most conniving creature that nature had ever concocted.

"This road's not even on the map," Frank said. "They probably built it after a washout. We'll have to re-map the whole thing from the base up."

The talk of unmapped roads, vultures and wolves...all in an area with no cell service—no way to call for help—had Ricky tense. What if something bad happened?

Ricky sidled up to Philippe.

"So, are there really things like wolves on the islands?"

Philippe was never fast with a response. "Well...I wouldn't worry about it."

"But are there? Here...on the island?"

With a slight smile on his face, Philippe said, "Well...it's this way. There are a lot of animals that can do you harm. The worst of them, they aren't the big ones like the bear and the lion, not that we have lions here, of course. The ones you've gotta watch out for are the little buggers. Do you know what animal poses the greatest risk to mankind? Guess."

Ricky thought for a moment. "Is it a wolf?"

"No, it's not the wolf."

"But a wolf could take a guy down, couldn't it?"

Philippe stared intently at Ricky. "Well...I suppose...but a wolf wouldn't rate nearly as dangerous as the tiny mosquito. Did you know that mosquito-borne illness takes almost a million lives every—"

"But say there was a wolf on the island," Ricky interrupted. "What kind would it be?"

"Well...I'd say it'd have to be the Grey Coastal. Yuh. There was one shot just the other year down on Vancouver Island. Now, speaking of which, it could be a Vancouver Island Wolf which is a subspecies of the Grey Coastal. I suppose one could have made it over to Marsh."

"So there could be two kinds of wolves around us right now?" Ricky said in a voice one step above a quivery whisper.

"You might be right. Better be glad you're not a lame deer or they could drop you in a second."

Just then there was a rustling in the bushes, and out leapt a large wolf. Or at least what Ricky imagined was what a wolf looked like. Without thinking, he pulled out a handgun, and fired off a half-dozen shots in the general direction of the wolf.

It was hard to say where the loudest noise came from—the gun, the men's yelling or Ricky's screaming, but the yelp of an injured animal rose above the rest. It quickly retreated into the brush.

"What the fuck?" Frank yelled as he grabbed the gun away from Ricky.

"I shot the wolf. Did you see that? I shot the fucking wolf!"

"Wolf? What wolf? There haven't been wolves on these islands for a hundred and fifty years."

"Well...not now there aren't. I just shot it!"

Frank hustled Ricky into the back seat of the truck.

"Where the fuck did you get that gun?" Frank yelled.

Ricky looked away. "I borrowed it...from my dad's collection in case..."

"Not only stupid, but illegal." Frank shook his head. "I'm going to have a long talk with your father when we get back."

Frank did the driving for the rest of the day. Ricky was ordered to stay in the truck and only leave if he had to pee.

* * * *

So, if you are one who believes that we can make a difference in this world by working together with one voice to save our wilderness, re-post this blog on any and all social media. And, if you are a supporter of West Coast Travel, Vancouver Island Publishing or Peak Capital Developments, reconsider your relationship. Their deception and hypocrisy cannot go unpunished.

To keep his social media readers on the hook, he let them know that more proof of outside collusion would be forthcoming. He didn't want to release the government connection too early. McCutcheon might be of more use in power than out of power. He could always bring down the corrupt politician later. In the meantime, someone would have to pay the Honourable Member of the Legislative Assembly a visit.

An Epilogue to his blog post took the form of a video, something he rarely did. For Rob, his work was, at its heart, not about him — it was about the people and the places he visited. The video he narrated consisted of a slideshow of islander's faces, each of whom would be drastically affected by the development. It was like the reading of names of victims of a disaster that put a human face on the attack. Was it manipulative? Rob hoped so.

He reviewed it one more time and pressed 'Post'. Rob had wielded the heaviest weapon in his arsenal — the power of thousands of rabid nature-lovers. Now he waited for the results. In the meantime, he added two more items to his list of assets.

He picked up his phone and called a number. The call was picked up on the third ring.

Rob said, "Look, I don't have much time. I need you to do me a favour."

"Sure. For you, anything."

He continued, "I'm going to email you a document and instructions. You once told me that you always wanted to try your hand at acting. Now's your chance."

"You got it."

"Thanks. I owe you big-time."

He disconnected and called a second number.

"Hey there. I need some help," Rob began.

"What is it, Robert?"

"I got to thinking about what you said the other day and it stung."

"Good. It was supposed to."

"I need some help to get out of the hole I'm in. Care to lend me a hand?" he asked.

"What do you need?"

"You know things no one else does. I need you to put that knowledge to good use."

He then painted in broad strokes what he needed to happen.

The ball was now starting to roll down the hill. He knew that there was no way to stop what he had put into motion.

In a matter of hours, his post and video had gone viral. His plea had ricocheted around the world and back again. He thought back on Cedric's comments about the cogs beginning to turn on the project. In the development process, he knew the next step would be to bring in the surveyors. If his plan didn't work quickly enough, he thought, there was one final salvo he could think of, and it was right out of Mitch's Aunt Sarah's playbook.

* * * *

Mitch hadn't seen Rufus in two days. Others had also commented on the dog's absence. He often wandered off for a day or two by himself, but not without someone spotting him gambolling across a field chasing a butterfly or sleeping under a tree by the side of the road.

Mitch got into his truck and had planned to scour the island looking for him. He knew of a favourite spot of Rufus', a small pond where, on hot days, the dog would wallow in the water to cool off and torment the frogs. It was just off the road to Admiral's Peak, about halfway up the mountain.

Mitch turned up the road. He noticed fresh tire tracks of a truck. Most likely it was the mayor. She often went up there to escape the hubbub of the town. Or maybe it was Sheila. She'd been known to come up here to release birds brought to her for healing. Maybe one of them had seen the dog. Best to stick to the road so he didn't miss them.

He continued up the track and something caught his eye. A pair of turkey vultures circled overhead, one spiralling down to land. On the island, one vulture was nothing to be concerned about. Two vultures meant...

He drove on for a moment, then, on the shoulder of the road, he noticed it — a vulture, picking at something. The second bird he had seen landed by it. The first let out a low, guttural hiss and flapped its wings, annoyed that it had been disturbed. Ignoring it, the second bird moved in to join the feast. It must have been a relatively large animal to attract two birds.

Mitch thought he knew what they were fighting over. He leapt from the truck and ran to the kill site, yelling and waving his arms. The birds were reluctant to give up their meal, but a few well-thrown rocks convinced them to move off.

Mitch slowly approached the dark mass that lay at the side of the road among the brush. Without looking closely, he knew what it was, but his heart prevented him from approaching any closer. He couldn't afford to lose anything else in his world. First Rob, then the island, then his brother and now...

He found his strength. If it was Rufus, he couldn't leave him for the vultures. He approached with fear and reverence as if he were a soldier approaching a fallen comrade.

It was Rufus. The dog had been badly picked over. Had he been hit by a car? Rufus had no sense of fear when it came to traffic. He was happy to see people and those came out of cars, didn't they? Rufus was dead and no matter the cause, Mitch knew what he had to do.

He walked back to the truck and pulled the dog's old blanket from the back seat. Mitch wrapped him up, carefully picked up his dearest friend and carried him back to the truck, where he laid him down in the cargo bed.

The procession to his final resting place was a slow and simple affair. Mitch drove carefully along the potholed road, up to where it ended. He took the shovel from the box and walked the rough path to below the rocky peak where he knew there was still enough soil to dig a grave. It was within view of Rufus' pond.

Once the hole was dug, he gathered his friend up in his arms and slowly walked up to the graveside where he lay Rufus to rest. To throw the first shovel of earth took every ounce of strength he had. He wept, and with each shovelful, his sobs grew deeper.

When the grave was filled, he was spent. How would he cope with being alone? He had relied for so long on the strength of others.

He knew one thing—he could not just give up. It would be the greatest insult to the memory of those who had worked to keep him alive when he'd given up on himself. He would have to go to the source of strength that saved him in the first place. He would go up the mountain as he had when he first arrived on the island. He would fast and meditate and, with time, he would have the answer.

Mitch climbed to the Peak and lay down.

Chapter Twenty

Francis waited at the ferry dock on Gabriola. It had been a slow day. The only passenger on his first trip to Marsh that morning was a nurse on her bicycle heading over to tend to Maggie Tupman's sunburn. The nurse, of course, didn't offer up that information. She was too professional to breach patient confidentiality, but everyone on the island knew anyway. Maggie had been laughing about it at the island council meeting the other day. She'd had to explain why she wouldn't sit down. The mayor always sat first. It was tradition. She had insisted that the others take their seats and she'd remain standing. She'd been out sunning herself and, as she said, "My bottom bore the brunt of the burn." Burned bottom or not, the council upheld tradition and remained standing for the entirety of the meeting.

No one came for the return trip to the mainland, as they referred to Gabriola, so Frances opted to tend to things in town while Francis managed the ferry single-handedly.

Just when it looked like there would be no traffic for the 10:15 a.m. sailing, a truck pulled up to the dock. The truck wasn't familiar, but the face of the driver was. Francis ambled to the driver's side.

"Mr Hanson. Didn't think we'd be seein' you in these parts again."

Rob looked uncomfortable. "Francis...I had a hundred things I was planning to tell your wife when I got here but..."

"Well...she ain't here."

"No...she isn't. Look, I know I screwed up, but I swear to you that I never meant any harm, to Mitch or any of you. I didn't do what Mitch thinks I did. And as far as that developer — I knew nothing about his plans. I was only here to write an article on the island."

"That so?" Francis muttered.

"Yes. It's the honest truth. I would never do anything to hurt Mitch, and I have a plan that just might save the island."

"Hm. You don't say?"

"If you'll just let me get over there, I'll prove it," Rob declared.

"You know, if my wife were here, she'd drive you and yer truck right off t'other side of this ferry before she'd let you near the island. She protects that boy o'er there like she'd protect her very own son."

Francis stood there weighing his options.

"But I'm not my wife, not that I don't love that boy — I'd be proud to call him my own — but after the way that politician McCutcheon and those surveyors treated us—"

Rob looked surprised. "The surveyors have arrived already?"

"Jus' the other day. Now, get on board."

"So, you believe me?"

"'Course I do. Unlike Frances, love 'er dearly, but she don' do her research. I just checked you up the o'er day at the café there," he said, pointing down the street. "I read yer blog. Subscribe to it too now, as a matter o' fact. Now get that tank o' yours onboard an' I'll get you o'er there. The survey crew's been stayin' at the inn, so they're probably up the mountain as we speak, doin' God-knows-what."

"Thank you, Francis. Thanks so much."

With ten minutes to go before the ferry was due to sail, Francis pulled away from the dock. It was the first time in the ferry's twenty-year history that the ship had ignored the sacred timetable. Before landing, Rob's rapidly evolving plan was in motion.

* * * *

Sheila Marsh filled up the tank of her GMC Yukon XL. She liked this truck. It had enough power to take her anywhere she needed to go and enough storage capacity for her veterinary equipment as well as a few dog crates. It even came in a pewter colour, which she found was best at hiding dirt.

As she was heading into the office to pay, a white Suburban drove by. That wasn't as surprising as the driver, whom she instantly identified as Rob Hanson. He was headed in the direction of Mitch Carcross' house.

She ran inside and tossed her credit card at Mike, the owner of Mike's Filling Station. "Ring up pump two for me, Mike, and can I use your phone?"

"Sure thing," Mike said, passing her the phone over the counter. She dialled Maggie Tupman's number.

"Maggie? Sheila here. Look, I'm not sure what's going on, but Rob Hanson's back in town and heading for Mitch's place. I'm gonna head up after him… I'm not sure if it has anything to do with the surveyors and the article he published, but I think he needs to know what's happening — with everything. It's time… Yeah. That might be a good idea. He might need some help with those surveyors. Or the other way around."

* * * *

Rob pulled up to Mitch's house. The truck was not in the driveway. He'd wait for Mitch to return. In the meantime, maybe now would be a good time to try and have a grown-up talk with Kevin.

He'd hoped Rufus would be around. He half expected to be bowled over by the big furry goofball once he stepped out of the truck, but the world was quiet.

Rob walked around the house to the side door. He was surprised to see it open. Not just opened, but propped open.

"Hello?"

There was no response. He stepped in. The place was a mess. Not like it had been rifled by burglars, just unkempt. Not like Mitch at all. He was so proud of his home.

"Kevin?"

Again, no response. Kevin wouldn't just be out. He never left the house. Rob had joked about it once. Kevin told him he couldn't leave. If he did, who'd protect his property?

Rob checked out the spare room where Kevin slept. It was empty. He walked slowly across the living room to Mitch's bedroom. The room that used to be theirs had an alien feeling. The bed was unmade. Clothes were scattered about. *Was this the way he lived before I came?* He couldn't convince himself of that. He had to check out the workshop. Maybe Mitch was there?

He stepped back into the living room and jumped when he saw Sheila in the doorway.

"Hello, Robert. I expected you to return."

"You did?"

"Yes." She looked at Rob with no emotion. It could also be said that she looked at him with no judgement either.

"He's not here," she said. "Neither of them is. Mitch kicked Kevin out."

Rob was dumbstruck. Mitch had stood up to him. His heart swelled with pride.

"So, what's going on?" Rob asked. "The door was wide open..."

"I think Mitch did that in case Rufus came back after he'd left."

"Where's Rufus?"

"No one knows. He left shortly after you did and no one's seen him since."

"And Mitch?"

Sheila took a deep breath. "Let me tell you a bit about that boy. There are some things you need to know."

"You already told me some things."

"You care for him, don't you?"

"I...love him," he confessed.

"Then you need to hear the rest."

Rob frowned. "Why are you doing this, after what people say I did?"

"I'm a doctor. I believe in facts, not in what the rumour mill churns out. That, and I did some research on you and I liked what I saw."

"I'm glad to hear it."

"Now, if you truly love that boy, you're going to have to take care of him, and to do that you will have to know more about him. What he's been through." She settled herself onto a kitchen stool.

"Sarah pulled him off the streets of Vancouver's East Hastings Street, a drug addict nearer death than life. She thought Mitch would have better luck recovering at her place than in a clinic. Mitch came to Sarah's a hollow shell. She saw him through the worst of the withdrawal.

"When he recovered enough, he told her that he needed to be alone for a while to find out who he really was. Sarah was spiritual enough to see the point, so she packed him food and a light sleeping bag—it was summer—and she took him to the Peak. She told him that if he was going to find himself, that would be the place. And she left him there.

"He had no strength. He told me later that he spent his hours thinking about his life and came to a realisation that there was nothing to go on for. His life had been a waste and his future held even less promise. What was the point of it all?

"By that point, he had eaten so little that he was all skin and bones. He decided to throw away the food and lay down on the blanket to starve himself. He remembered hallucinating. An ancient person, man or woman, he couldn't tell, came to him. The ancient fed him a mash of berries, grubs, mushrooms and insects. They talked to him about the gift of life and that as long as there was life there was the chance to do good, to reward those that have loved him in the past and love him now."

"Do you believe that story?" he asked.

"Of course I do. I was there when Sarah fed him."

"Sarah was the ancient one? Did she really feed him berries, grubs and insects?"

"Of course she did. It was high-protein, high-sugar diet. Just what his system needed."

"So Sarah...she was a..." Rob searched for the right word, not wanting to offend.

"Let's just say she had a lot of wisdom."

"And she was able to heal him?"

"As much as she could. What had the strongest healing power was a faith in nature, the island and, most importantly the Peak, which is where I suspect he's gone again to heal the damage done by these recent events."

"When did you last see him?" Rob asked.

"A week ago. If I were you, I'd head up soon."

"What do I do when I find him?"

"You'll know what to do."

Rob ran out the door, got into his truck and made his way to the Peak. He drove carefully up the winding road. On the hairpin turn he noticed something that disturbed him—a wooden stake wrapped in orange flagging tape had been driven into the ground. Without warning, the surveyors had launched the first salvo in the battle for the island.

Chapter Twenty-One

It had been a long flight from Toronto and a short time to freshen up and get dressed. She wore her best black dress — simple, clingy, and ending just below the knees. On her feet she wore her black Manolo Blahnik Hangisi knock-off pumps. Karen made her way along Fort Street searching for the address. Why had she not taken a cab? Why had she chosen these shoes? Sure, they were drop-dead gorgeous, but why was beauty so pinchy?

She thought that a long-time Member of Parliament would have a nicer office — maybe one in the legislative building, or at least a pretty, older building near it. The office at 1052 Fort Street was on the second floor above a music instrument store, and not an affluent one at that.

Having manoeuvred her way up the uneven wooden stairs, she reached a small landing with a single door straight out of a Sam Spade movie. It was dark wood with a frosted glass window. Above it was a transom window covered in enough coats of paint to make it impossible to open. The window bore a hand-painted sign indicating that this was the Office of Hugh McCutcheon Esq., MLA, Salish-North Islands.

Karen knocked. Nothing. She knocked louder. Nothing. She was about to try a third time when the door opened.

On the other side of the door stood a portly older man with slicked-back grey hair. He was dressed in an old, dark-grey three-piece suit with a bright party-blue necktie. On his face he wore a scowl which rapidly turned into a broad grin. *This is the guy,* she thought. *And he ain't Bogart.*

"Well, hello, young lady. Hugh McCutcheon at your service."

The politician stuck out his hand, which she took.

"Please. Do come in."

He led her in with the hand that held hers. The other hand he placed on her lower back just above her buttocks. He kicked the door closed with his foot.

"Please forgive my delay in answering the door. My secretary is off for the day." McCutcheon paused for a moment, lost in thought. "Actually, she's off for the next month as the legislature isn't sitting. No point in paying someone to sit around with nothing to do except answer the phone and door. I may look old enough to be your grandfather, but I'm still able to do the basics when it comes to running an office."

He escorted her to a seat in his inner office. By the time she was ready to sit, McCutcheon's hand had drifted southward to rest on Karen's backside. She took advantage of the proffered chair and quickly sat.

"Now, what can I do for you, young lady?"

"Well, Mr McCutcheon, I've always been interested in politics. I can't think of a more honourable and selfless career — to serve others."

She made a conscious decision to inhale deeply at this point. His eyes had been focused on her breasts at the time.

"I can't agree with you more, Miss…?"

Miss? Karen hadn't thought far enough ahead to come up with a false identity.

It was amazing how quickly the brain could work when under pressure utilising the environment and recent events. Her life became a video in reverse — her sitting down, his hand on her ass, him taking her by the hand, the door opening, the door, Sam Spade… What was his secretary's name?

"Oh, I'm sorry. Effie Perrine, but you can call me Effie."

"Well, Effie. What can I do for you?"

"Well…I know you're a very busy man…"

"No problem at all, my dear. Just tell me what's on your mind?"

"Well, I thought to myself, if you have a question about how politics works, go to someone with experience."

"An excellent idea."

"And I know that you've been in the game for decades — not that I'm saying you're old."

"Oh, but I am, my dear. I am. Sometimes I feel like I've been around since the signing of the British-North America Act." He laughed at his own little joke.

"Well, I wouldn't worry. You don't look any older than VE Day," she rallied, thinking it a compliment.

"That was in 1945, if I'm not mistaken. I was born in 1949," he replied, dejected.

"Sorry."

"Well, enough chatting. I have a busy schedule today. What exactly are you interested in?"

The Right Honourable Member took the seat opposite Karen.

"Well, to be honest...I finally discovered politics! Yeah, wild, huh? There are so many things I don't understand."

She leaned forward a little to give him a better view of her cleavage.

"W-well, feel free to ask me anything, my dear. I'm here to educate and serve." He laughed.

"Well, like I said, I'm a little new to politics, so I don't know all the rules yet, but I was wondering if someone in government, let's say, I don't know, a city alderman, offered to do you a big favour if you did him a favour in return — would that be legal?"

"Well...I suppose it would depend on the type of favour he was being asked to do and the favour he was expecting in return."

"Oh," she answered, sounding a little confused. "How about, if a constituent asked the alderman for help in having a tree planted in his neighbourhood park in exchange for a little plaque thanking the alderman for his assistance, then there would be no problem with that, would there?"

"No. There'd be nothing wrong in that act of gratitude. It would be quite nice of someone to do something like that," he said. "But if that same alderman blocked passage of a zoning bill in order to prevent the construction of, let's say subsidised housing in that same neighbourhood in exchange for a large campaign donation... Well, that would be another thing altogether."

"Well, that's what I thought. So, it seems that the wrongfulness rides on how much the alderman benefits from the deal."

"That, young lady, sums it up nicely."

"So, what about this case then?"

Karen pulled out the copy Rob had made of the letter he had taken from Cedric's office. She handed it to McCutcheon.

"In your experience, would this be evidence suggesting an unlawful act was being perpetrated that would warrant investigation?"

As the politician began to read the letter, Karen reached into her purse and extracted her phone.

He was slow to recognise the document at first, but as he read the letter, his hands began to shake. When Karen saw him reach the stage of shifting uncomfortably in his chair and licking his lips as if they would no longer function, she pressed 'Play' on her phone's audio playback function.

"What kind of idiot puts that sort of thing in writing? Do you have any idea what would happen if those fools on the island got a hold of something like this? And on Ministry letterhead? Really! ...Honestly, McCutcheon, if you hadn't picked up the bar tabs for half of your constituents, I don't think you would ever have been elected. We'll talk about this later."

"Would you like to hear that again, Mr McCutcheon?" Karen offered.

"Wh...what's the meaning of this? You barge in like this and...and... This is clearly a case of extortion and I won't stand for it!"

"Extortion implies an unwanted request for payment in exchange for something in return."

"You have implied a threat!"

"I have asked for nothing, merely shown you a letter and played you a bit of a speech. Nothing more. How you choose to interpret it... Well, that's up to you, Mr McCutcheon."

Karen stood to leave.

"Oh, no need to show me out. And you can keep that," she added, pointing to the letter. "I have other copies."

With an unnatural, dignified poise, Karen departed, closing the door behind her. The only sounds that followed were that of objects being hurled across McCutcheon's office, and the clattering of Manolo Blahnik knock-offs on worn, wooden stairs.

Once again in the Victoria sunshine, Karen screamed with excitement, grabbing a passing businessman in a frenzied dance of triumph. She let go of his arm, and continued down the street, leaving him standing there with a confused smile on his face.

* * * *

Marco was a master at extracting sediment cores. He backed the soil sampling rig, which was attached to the back of the truck, up to the edge of the roadbed. No one, not even Frank, would dare to offer to help do this. It wasn't a difficult manoeuvre—the rig wasn't particularly large—but Marco was particular in its positioning. He had a sixth sense when it came to drilling. He always knew where the most unstable soil could be found, which meant he was always cautious — a trait desirable in a driller boring a one-hundred-foot deep, six-inch-wide core, in the hope that it would prove that the road would hold the weight of a cement truck.

Marco was only satisfied when the rig was within a few feet of the slope of the mountain, which left the truck blocking the narrow roadway.

"Should I be worrying about this?" Marco yelled to Frank.

"Nah. It doesn't look like the road's been used in a while. As long as we get things looking organised for the chopper fly-over later this morning. They don't want the investors to see a mess."

"You've gotta be—"

"Don't go there."

When Marco finessed the rig into position, Ricky leapt in behind the truck and started unhitching the drill frame to raise it into the upright drilling position as he'd seen Marco do.

"Get your fuckin' hands off that," Marco yelled, grabbing Ricky by the shoulders and throwing him through the air.

"What the fuck, man? I was just giving you a hand."

"Best not to touch another man's tools." Frank laughed.

"Shit. That guy's crazy," Ricky shouted, pumped up on adrenaline.

"You pull that pin, kid, and the whole drill frame will flip up and take your goddamn head off."

"Yeah...well..." Ricky walked away.

Philippe came up to Frank. "Kid gonna be okay?"

"The one thing they hate more than being told what to do is being told they did something wrong. Nothing worse for a twenty-year-old, not that you'd remember," Frank added, laughing.

Philippe laughed. "Crap—I can't even remember *being* twenty."

"Just watch him. He'll be showing off just to prove he's a real man," Frank cautioned.

Marco loaded the six-inch-wide drill auger into the drive and raised the drill frame carefully into position. Every move Marco made was measured.

Just then, a white Suburban drove around the corner and skidded to a halt.

* * * *

At 11:35 a.m., Estelle slowly mounted the stairs of the Broughton Street offices of Vancouver Island Publishing. Her office might have been in an old building, but at least it had an elevator. *Strike two, Cedric.*

As she waited outside the office to catch her breath, she could hear the phone ring. Although she couldn't quite make out the words spoken, she could sense the tone, and it was one of frustration. Estelle entered as the telephone receiver was slammed down. No sooner than the receptionist looked up to see who had entered, the phone rang again. The receptionist grabbed at the receiver like it was a snake ready to strike.

"I have no idea what you are talking about," she yelled and slammed the receiver back on the cradle before the caller had a chance to utter a syllable.

"It's been like that all morning. Is there some new disease going around that makes people go crazy? Should I be thinking about getting a shot?"

The phone rang again and Brenda picked up and slammed the receiver right back down. "I've been having people who don't even speak English yelling at me. That's not right, is it?"

"I have no idea. I'm here to see Cedric."

"Do you have an—" Before she could finish the sentence the phone rang again. "Oh, just go in," she said, waving the receiver towards the inner office door. "What!" she yelled into the phone. "Sorry, Mom, I didn't know it was you... No, I don't always answer the phone like that."

With that, Estelle entered Cedric's office. She noticed his phone lay on the floor some ten feet from the end of its cord.

"I'm too busy right now, so would you please leave," he said without looking up.

"But Cedric darling, it's been a very long flight," she said, in a way that would have made a 1930s screen vamp proud.

"Estelle! What are you doing here, my love?"

"The mountain comes to Mohamed." Estelle walked to his desk and hoisted her short frame onto the edge of his desk.

"My dear, I'm afraid you've come at an inopportune time. As you probably sensed, things are a little...chaotic at the moment."

"Yes, I couldn't help but see that. Who knew that the travel publishing business could be so...active?"

"Oh, my dear, you have no idea. No idea at all." He finally rose from his chair and leaned in for a kiss but Estelle swivelled off the desk and back onto her feet.

"I had a meeting with one of my clients," she said as she sauntered to the window overlooking a quaint little café across the street. She would treat herself to a nice coffee when this was done. "He was surprised at the number of cuts you made to his article."

"Well, the article was a rather lengthy one, as I recall. And he did sign a contract that stipulated the editor's right to make cuts for reason of size."

"Size, yes, but not in such a way as to change the author's viewpoint. And when did you start dealing with the writers directly when they have competent representation? I hope you haven't lost faith in my abilities, Cedric?" she said with just the right wounded tone to her voice.

He moved in to reassure her.

"No, my dear. Nothing of the sort. It was merely a matter of timing. If we were going to get the piece into the next issue we had to act quickly." He placed his arms around her waist, pulling her close. "And every...second...counted." As he bent to kiss her, she drove her epoxy-hardened talons into his crotch, grasping onto his low-hanging fruit like an eagle onto a fish, and twisted.

Cedric's scream was only drowned out by Brenda's shout of "I quit!" and the sound of her phone hitting the inner office door.

"If I ever hear of you manipulating another article for the sake of promoting your other business ventures, I will go to your wife with everything you've been up to, and I mean everything. And don't forget—I have the videos to prove it. She'll cut you off without a dime...and your precious balls."

Estelle stormed out through the empty outer office and across the street where she treated herself to a lovely French roast. As she sat and sipped her coffee, she smiled. It had been a long flight, but it had been worth it to see the look on his face. No one took advantage of one of her clients like that and got away with it.

She had planned on catching flight 8076 to Toronto via Vancouver, but realised that if she stopped off in that city for a few days, she could touch base in person with a few film people she knew. She had an idea that she wanted to run by them. Besides, it would make it easier to write the trip off. After all, costs associated with taking revenge on a badly behaved ex-lover were not covered by the Canada Revenue Agency as deductible expenses.

Chapter Twenty-Two

"Jesus! Put out some safety cones for Christ's sake. Are you trying to kill someone?" Rob screamed from the truck which he managed to stop a few yards from the drilling rig.

"Ricky! Did you put out the cones like I told you to?" yelled Frank, who had just barely been able to leap out of the way.

"I was going to do it after I helped Marco."

"Fucking idiot," Frank mumbled as he walked over to Rob's Suburban. "Hey, look, buddy, I'm sorry about that. Are you okay?"

"Yeah," Rob said. He was still gripping the steering wheel.

"Sorry, I got this new kid working with me. Sometimes I don't think his head's screwed on right.

"Ricky, stop starin' and put out those cones *now!*"

Ricky begrudgingly pulled some orange safety cones off the mount welded to the front bumper of the truck. He walked them past Rob's truck, not making eye contact with anyone. They could hear him throwing them down one by one when he was around the corner out of sight.

Rob stepped out of the Suburban.

Frank stood his ground. "We'll get the truck out of the way as soon as the drill rig is secured. It'll just take a few minutes."

"Good. I'm in a bit of a rush."

"No fucking kidding," Ricky mumbled as he walked past, back towards the truck.

"Jerk," Rob muttered.

"What the fuck did you say?" Ricky yelled, pumped up on the humiliation he was fed by the others.

Rob felt the tension in the air. He sussed out the situation. The kid didn't look like a fighter, but the runt of the litter was often the one you had to watch out for.

The kid approached him. His eyes were on fire. His upper lip curled like a mad dog's. This kid had a fight building inside him and he was going to let it out.

"What's wrong, little man? Not feeling so strong outside of your big truck?"

"Ricky!" Frank snapped, but Ricky wasn't hearing anything. He was locked in on the one guy he thought he could beat, and he was going to make him pay.

The boy shoved Rob by the shoulder. Rob almost lost his balance. He could fight back, but if the others got into the fray, he'd be a goner.

Ricky shoved again.

"What's wrong, faggot? That's it, isn't it? You're a faggot. Stop looking at me, faggot."

At that moment, a voice came from behind.

"Watch that mouth of yours, you little asshole!"

Maggie Tupman came into view.

"Hey, faggot, you need your granny to come to your rescue?"

"Granny? Why, you little shit." Maggie was angry and Ricky was in trouble, even though he didn't know it.

"Ricky! Shut that goddammed mouth of yours and get back to the truck," Frank yelled.

"No! I am so sick and tired of everyone telling me what to do. My dad owns this company. He owns all of you. That makes me your boss. I'll do the talking from now on."

The kid has lost it, Rob thought.

"And that goes for you, too, grandma."

"I'd watch what you say, little man. That's the mayor you're talking to," another voice added.

Rob turned around to see Eric rounding the corner, followed by Sheila…and a few dozen islanders.

"You call someone a faggot, I take it personal." Eric approached Ricky. He stood a head taller than the boy and outweighed him by a good sixty pounds. A look of terror filled Ricky's eyes.

"Something you want to say, you little pussy?"

By this point, there was almost thirty people filling the road.

"All right. Everybody, just take a deep breath." Frank tried to take control of the situation. "Ricky, get back to the truck. Now, while you still have your balls."

Ricky slid between Eric and the mayor and ran back to the safety of the truck.

"Now, let's just…"

"You seem to be planning to do some drilling here," Maggie said.

"That's pretty much what we do."

Ricky stood by the front of the truck with Marco and Philippe.

"This doesn't look good," Philippe said.

"I coulda finished this off before it started." Ricky moved away to the back of the truck and crawled in.

"You know, you need a permit to be drilling on the mountain road."

"We've got better than that. We've got government approval."

"Not from this level of government," Maggie said, stepping forward. "And I don't see that lily-livered Hugh McCutcheon anywhere around here, do you?"

All throughout her speech the islanders moved forward, slowly surrounding the survey crew.

"On the island here, we have a history of living by our own rules. And one of those is the protection of the mountain as a sacred site. I don't think McCutcheon would fare well in the next election if he was caught supporting Peak Capital Developments' destruction of a sacred site, do you?"

"All right, that's it!" Ricky yelled. Rob had been so mesmerised by the confrontation he had not noticed that to his right Ricky had climbed up on the drill rig with a rifle which he was now pointing at the crowd.

"All of you, get back. Now!"

"Fuck. He's got the crew rifle from the back of the truck," Marco said.

"Ricky, are you crazy? Put that thing down," yelled Frank, who was now white with fear.

"You've screwed this up from the start, Frank. Now it's time to let a real man deal with it."

Rob later remembered what happened next as happening in slow motion and almost absolute silence. Only key sounds seemed to register. Out of the corner of his eye he saw a dark shape moving silently through the brush to his left. No one else seemed to see it. All eyes were on the boy.

"I said move it. Now!" Ricky yelled.

Everyone stood in silence.

The dark figure moved on, seemingly unconcerned or unaware of what was happening around it as it continued through the woods. There was a crack of brittle wood. Rob saw Ricky's eyes move to the same spot he was looking at. It was then that Rob recognised the shape for what it was — Mitch!

"Bear!" yelled Ricky. "Bear!" he screamed as he raised his rifle.

"No," yelled Rob as he dove between Mitch and the gun. Time almost stopped. The sound of the explosion of the gun. The searing pain. He heard Maggie scream as he hit the ground. Rob could taste the soil in his mouth. That was the last thing he remembered as things went black.

No one saw the figure in the woods which ran back into the bush at the sound of the gunshot.

* * * *

Sheila recognised the spray of arterial blood from Rob's thigh before he hit the ground.

"Somebody get me a first-aid kit," she yelled as she ran to Rob. "*Now!*"

She placed her thumbs on both sides of the wound and pressed hard. The wound kept leaking blood, and lots of it. The bullet must have nicked the femoral artery. If it had severed it, there would be even more blood, if that was possible. She shifted her thumbs and the blood flow lessened. There. The bleeding subsided, but she couldn't keep the pressure up for long. She needed —

"Eric! Get your ass over here."

Eric pushed his way through the crowd that had formed around Rob. Philippe, with the crew's first-aid kit, followed in his wake.

"Everybody back up and give us room," Eric yelled, then knelt beside Sheila. "Holy shit," he muttered.

Sheila looked him in the eye and whispered, "Keep it together." She knew that everyone around them was scared. She had to maintain control. In a loud enough voice so all could hear, she firmly said, "Eric, you're gonna have to use those muscles of yours. Put your thumbs on the outside of mine and push down like I am."

Eric hesitated.

"Just do as I'm doing and he'll be just fine."

Eric mimicked her position.

"Okay. I'm going to remove my thumbs and you slide your two thumbs closer together like I had them." Eric did as he was told and the transfer went perfectly. "Okay. You're good. Let me know if you need a break."

Sheila wrapped the leg as best she could and indicated that Eric needed to keep the pressure on.

Eric's muscles trembled as he tried to save Rob's life. His T-shirt darkened with sweat.

Sheila stood. She could hear Ricky at the back of the crowd say, "It was a bear! Did you see it?"

"Bear? I haven't seen a bear on this island for thirty years," Sheila said. "We need to get him to a hospital now. Any ideas?"

"We could use the ferry, but I don't think it'll be fast enough," said Frances, her voice breaking as she held back her tears.

"We're going to have to get him to Nanaimo. Their hospital is the closest with a trauma centre."

Maggie yelled at Frank, "You—does your truck have a radio?"

"Yeah. Wait...there's a chopper on its way here for a tour. It could fly him there. What's the nearest spot one could touch down?"

"The Peak!" Maggie responded. "It's a bald knob. Nothing to get in its way."

"We'll take him there," said Frank. "Guys, unhook the rig and clear out the back of the truck."

Philippe and Marco leapt to it.

"And someone get that fuckin' gun away from the kid," Frank said as he ran to the truck to radio for help.

"We'll need something we can use as a stretcher," Sheila added.

Marco was already dumping soil samples from a long wooden core box. "This'll do," he said, running it over to Eric's side.

"We'll need to make sure that Eric can maintain pressure on the wound when we lift him onto the crate." Sheila coordinated the move with the help of Marco, Philippe and a couple of the strongest islanders. They were able to get Rob onto the makeshift stretcher without too much additional blood loss.

As they carried the body to the truck, Ricky piped up with a "Hey, can I give a hand?" Maggie and a few others who had been watching as Rob's blood-soaked, ashen face was whisked by took Ricky by the arms and pulled him away.

"The chopper will be there in five minutes," Frank reported.

"I was aiming for the bear. He ran in the way. You all saw it. It wasn't my fault. He got in the way. I was trying to save you all from the bear before it attacked."

"Someone put him in a car," Maggie ordered. "We'll lock him up at my place until the RCMP can get here."

Eric never for a moment released pressure on the wound as Rob was placed carefully in the back of the truck. Sheila crawled into the cargo area with them as the guys who carried the stretcher joined Frank up front for the cautious drive up to the Peak.

* * * *

Maggie and Francis took Ricky, who sat in the back of Maggie's car, hands bound with gauze bandaging, back to Maggie's house where they locked him in the large pantry with a ham sandwich and glass of milk.

"You did see it, didn't you?"

"What?" Francis asked.

"The bear? It was huge, wasn't it?"

Neither of them answered.

* * * *

Back on the mountain road, Frances waited until the others had gone, and the helicopter had flown overhead. *Things are in God's hands now,* she thought. The islanders had done all they could.

She walked back to her car and reflected on what had happened that afternoon. She wasn't the kind of person who was brought to tears often but, once she had seated herself in her old Mini, she began to cry. She pictured that poor boy running towards the brush, for what reason, who knew? And the other one, the one who seemed to be simple, who pulled the trigger...and for what? A bear? Like Sheila had said — there hadn't been a bear on the island for decades. *What could he have been goin' on about?*

She started the car and slowly made her way down Peak Road.

* * * *

In the fog that enveloped his brain, Mitch remembered hearing what he thought was a crowd of people, of someone yelling "Bear," followed by what sounded like a gunshot. Was someone hunting on the island? That didn't make sense.

He longed for solitude and apparently, he was not going to find it here. He moved down the mountain, away from the sound of the people he did not see, or care to. Away from the helicopter buzzing overhead. Away from the Peak. He took it as a sign—it was time to go home, a place where he could reflect on all he had experienced while up on the mountain.

* * * *

Mitch walked into his house and looked around. He vaguely remembered leaving the door open. He wandered around, taking in the rooms, picking up a few items here and there, putting them back in place or tossing them out onto the porch—like Rufus' old blanket by the fireplace, and a few of Kevin's things. He had no need for them now. He came across one of Rob's sweaters. It was the soft grey one knit from merino wool. He was about to throw it out when he gave it a second thought and put it on. He was cold.

He went into the kitchen and threw most of the food out. It was time to start over. He found an apple that he devoured and a piece of cheese that hadn't gone mouldy yet. Everything else was either there because of Rob or Kevin.

The cleaning went on until late in the evening when, after lighting a fire and pouring himself a glass of wine, Mitch settled into his chair and watched the flames dance.

As a child, he could watch fires for hours. They were alive, always changing. They offered both comfort and pain, provided security and destruction. His father would joke that he and Mitch's mom wondered if they should be concerned about whether they were raising an arsonist.

While staring into the flames, he thought of his last week on the mountain, surviving on spring water and the occasional meal of berries and mushrooms. He remembered the hallucinations, including a huge house party. He remembered being visited by his Aunt Sarah. She told him to trust her and…something else. He couldn't put his finger on it. It was like a memory that was at the tip of his tongue. An idea he couldn't quite visualise. He also remembered her walking with him, her putting her arms around him and telling him to go back home. Not quite that, though. He stared into the flames and remembered her face staring at him. She said, "Go back and *make* yourself a home." That was different, but right now, he had no idea where to begin.

Chapter Twenty-Three

The helicopter was waiting for Frank and his crew when they arrived. The investors, having been apprised of the situation, were more than willing to be abandoned on the Peak knowing that a life was at stake and that they would have a great story to dine out on for the next year.

Marco, Philippe, Frank and Sheila were able to manoeuvre the makeshift stretcher into the cabin of the helicopter as Eric maintained pressure on the wound. Even with all of his strength, Eric was finding it difficult, but he refused to be beaten.

The helicopter took off with Sheila, Eric and the patient. The survey crew ferried the investors back into town for an exciting night at the Marsh Inn. Within fifteen minutes, the helicopter was landing at the Nanaimo Regional General Hospital's heliport with a full trauma team on stand-by.

Sheila had monitored Rob's vitals as best she could during the flight.

"His breathing is shallow, his pulse is weak, and he's lost a lot of blood," she shouted over the roar of the rotors as they unloaded Rob from the helicopter.

"Are you the attending physician?" yelled one of the hospital team to Sheila.

"No, I'm a vet."

"Army?"

"Dog and cat, mostly. But I'm certified for large animals."

Both Sheila and Eric were relieved of their duties and the medical team quickly wheeled Rob into the hospital and into the trauma centre.

"There's nothing more we can do. Can I buy you a coffee?" Sheila asked Eric.

"No. But you can buy me the biggest drink this town has to offer."

The Windward Pub was a two-minute walk away.

After a good meal and several stiff drinks, they made their way back to the hospital. There was still nothing to report. Rob was in critical, but stable condition. Sheila gave them her contact information if anything changed. They gave her directions to the nearest hotel where the two checked in for the night.

Eric spent the first two hours in the hotel spa hot tub trying to relax his arm and hand muscles. Afterwards he picked up a waiter from the bar and took him back to his room for further de-stressing.

In the morning, Sheila met up with Eric in the restaurant where the waiter was overly attentive, even to the point of calling him 'hun.'

"What did you do to him?"

"Do you really want to know?"

"Probably not."

They took their coffees to go and headed back to the hospital.

Rob had undergone surgery the evening before and was in intensive care. No visitors allowed. They waited for an hour before being able to meet with a doctor, a young resident—Martin Quinn.

"Is one of you his next-of-kin?" he asked.

Eric looked him in the eye. "Nope. We're just the ones who saved his life."

"We're friends of Rob. We haven't had time to notify his family," Sheila added.

"Would that include a...Mitchell Carcross?" the doctor asked after referring to his chart.

"There's a long story there," Sheila answered.

"Mr Hanson insisted on us witnessing an entirely illegible written statement leaving Mr Carcross everything if he didn't make it." He showed them a piece of paper with a few intersecting scribbles on it. "He wrote that this morning when he came out of surgery. I don't think it would hold up in court. He was pretty stoned on meds at the time."

"Now, why can't I find someone like that?" Eric sighed.

"How extensive were the damages, Doctor?" Sheila asked.

"I understand it was a gunshot wound?"

"Yes," Sheila confirmed.

"It seems the bullet nicked the femoral artery before passing through the leg and out the back. It appears that you got the bleeding under control quickly, although there was still significant blood loss. What was Mr Hanson doing at the time?"

"Saving a bear from a gun nut. You know—real manly stuff," Eric quipped, with a broad smile. "I kept pressure on the wound until we got here. I guess all those hours at the gym paid off." Eric flexed his biceps. It did the trick. Dr Quinn giggled.

Sheila asked, "Will we be able to see him?"

"Once he's out of danger and moved up onto a ward."

"How long until he's released?"

"It's too soon to tell. He's very lucky you were with him. If you weren't, he would have died."

* * * *

It was early morning when there was a knock on Maggie's door. She opened it to find two strangers wearing the operational uniforms of the RCMP — blue pants with a gold stripe, grey shirt under a blue Gore-Tex patrol jacket. The older male had three chevrons on the arm designating him as a sergeant. The younger female's coat bore the double chevron of a corporal.

"Sergeant. Corporal." She nodded in welcome.

"Maggie Tupman?" said the older male.

"The one and only."

"I'm Sergeant Crawley. This is Corporal Evans from the Gabriola Island detachment." Maggie shook their hands.

"Come on in. I have coffee brewing if you have time for a cup."

As they entered, Corporal Evans' eyes checked with her superior, who smiled.

"I think that's a yes from my corporal."

"And for the sergeant?"

"It would be rude to have her drink alone."

Maggie led them into the kitchen of her modest two-storey home. It was a utilitarian structure with little in the way of the bric-a-brac that one would have expected from an eighty-year-old woman. The kitchen, however, was obviously the heart of this home. Counters covered in baking dishes and Tupperware containers, tins of flour and canning jars, empty and full, filled the shelves and surfaces.

Maggie poured out two mugs of coffee.

"Cream and sugar's on the table, and help yourselves to these," she said, putting out a plate of fresh-baked cookies. "Don't worry, they're not as bad for you as they look."

Evans took a long draw on her black coffee and helped herself to a couple of the cookies.

"God, these are good." She sighed.

Crawley laughed, helping himself to a cookie. "Not like the packaged ones at the station."

"I'll send you the recipe," Maggie offered.

"Thanks, but right now, we're here on official business. I understand that you have taken a man into custody," Crawley said.

"Yes. He's in my storage room."

Maggie walked them out of the kitchen towards the back of the house.

"What I know is the boy's name is Ricky and he accidentally shot a friend of mine, claiming he was aiming at a bear that he thought was going to attack him."

"I understand the victim is in critical but stable condition in Nanaimo."

"That's what I hear. I hope for everyone's sake he pulls through," Maggie added.

As she unlocked the door, the officers went to unholster their Smith and Wesson 3953 sidearms.

Maggie looked at them and said, "I don't think you'll be needing those."

Maggie opened the door to reveal Ricky sitting on a small, upholstered armchair, eating some of Maggie's cookies. A large mug of hot chocolate sat on the side table alongside the remains of a full breakfast.

"Are they here to arrest me?" Ricky said nervously.

"Yes," Maggie replied.

"Well, it seems like you've been treating him well," Crawley noted.

"As mayor and sole law enforcement officer on the island I felt it was my duty to put the island's best foot forward."

"You don't have a jail cell on Marsh?" Evans asked.

"You're looking at it. It's probably the reason I was elected. Seems like I was the only one with a spare room with a lock on the door."

Sergeant Crawley placed Ricky in handcuffs.

"I suppose they're mandatory?" Maggie asked.

"Yup," Crawley said.

Ricky turned to Maggie. "I didn't mean to cause any trouble."

"Just you behave yourself with these fine people."

Crawley led him out of the house.

Maggie picked up Ricky's dishes and took them into the kitchen.

"I was sorry to hear about Mr Hanson," Corporal Evans said. "I met him once at the detachment office. He seemed like a nice guy. I just had word that he's been cleared on that whole African charge."

"Africa? Do I want to hear about this?" Maggie replied, handing Evans a Tupperware box. "Here. Have some more cookies for the road."

Maggie walked the corporal to her cruiser. Ricky was secured in the back seat in handcuffs. He nodded to her through the window. Maggie waved back.

"And, Corporal, make sure you give some of those cookies to Ricky."

* * * *

There was a loud thump at the door. Mitch woke with a start. He was still in his chair. There was a second thump.

"Just a minute," he mumbled, then tried to stand. His neck was kinked, and his back felt like he had slept on a rock and... Why did his mouth taste like... *What* did his mouth taste like?

He opened the door to find Maggie, her arms loaded with groceries.

"Frances told me someone noticed your lights on last night and figured you'd come home. I thought you could use these. You unpack and I'll talk."

"Sure. Thanks for all this."

Mitch took the bags from her and she settled down on one of the stools in the kitchen.

"So, were you up on the mountain?" Maggie asked.

"Yeah. I got a lot of thinking done. Coffee?"

"Love some."

Mitch was noted for, among many other things, making some of the best coffee on the island.

"So...did you hear anything when you were up there yesterday?" Maggie inquired. "Any...ruckus?"

"I thought I heard a gunshot. Was someone hunting up there?" he answered. He sensed that something was up. Maggie was acting very strange. "Is there something I should know about?"

"Is it too late to change the coffee order to something stronger?" she replied.

"Scotch work for you?"

"If it's big enough."

Mitch poured her a double, then poured one for himself. They moved into the living room and Mitch lit a fire.

"This is nice." Maggie sighed, stretching out her feet towards the fire and wiggling her toes. "Is it just me, or are the nights getting a bit cooler around here?" She sat and looked at the flames for a moment before she said, "Rob came back looking for you."

Mitch looked at her with confusion. "He did? When?"

"Yesterday."

"I'm surprised Frances let him onto the ferry."

"She didn't. Francis did."

Mitch was surprised. Why would he do that given the fact that Rob had stabbed them all in the back when he'd chosen Craddock over them?

"It seems he's been keeping his eye on your Rob—"

"He's not mine!" Mitch interrupted.

"Well, Francis has been keeping an eye on Rob since he left. It seems he has a blog."

"Some people like to hear themselves talk."

"It appears a lot of people like to hear that boy talk," Maggie continued. "Thousands of people, according to Francis."

"It's a free world I guess."

"His last post was about being scammed by a real estate developer into promoting the destruction of an island habitat. Seems the developer edited the article he wrote, changing it to look like Rob was in support of the plan."

Mitch got up and adjusted a log on the fire with a poker. "Sure. That's what he says now."

"He's got almost fifty-thousand signatures on a petition protesting the development."

"Well, we'll never know what the original article said, will we?"

Maggie looked surprised. "He never showed it to you?"

"I asked and he said it wasn't ready yet. Then he had the balls to use my computer to type it up."

"Yeah, I see why you'd feel — wait a minute. He used your computer? Did he delete the file?"

He thought about it. "I don't know."

"Do yourself a favour and, before you write him off, look for it and read it. Now!"

Mitch respected Maggie. She was always supportive of him. In spite of the feelings he had towards Rob, he searched for the computer.

Where was it? He looked around the living room. That was where he normally left it, but it wasn't there. Maybe Kevin had used it and left it somewhere else. *Snooping again,* he thought. But it wasn't in the spare room. He walked through the living room to his bedroom. Maggie just sat and watched.

There, on his dresser, was the laptop. Beside it, in a cheap glass vase, was the paper flower Rob had made for him. He picked it up and smelled it. When Mitch had placed it in the vase, he'd insisted on giving it a light spray of Rob's cologne. So few men wore cologne anymore. It was so…last century. But on Rob…it was heavenly. What was it? *"Something my sister gave me a few Christmases ago,"* he'd said. 'Straight to Heaven', that was it. They'd laughed about the name. *"Straight — I bet you the only people who wear it are gay men."* His heart swelled, and he wiped away a tear and placed the flower back in the vase. He looked at the laptop and headed back into the living room without it.

"I have no idea where that damned computer is. Kevin probably stole it. Why are you so on Rob's side when he tried to destroy your home?"

"I...I just have this gut feeling he's not who you think he is. Oh — one thing you might want to know. I had a chat with the RCMP from Gabriola. They said that Rob had been cleared of any and all charges that stemmed out of some African event. Does that mean anything to you? Sounded like it must have been some odd misunderstanding."

Mitch rubbed his face hard.

"Yeah. Another odd misunderstanding."

* * * *

Maggie left with much unsaid.

She saw that Mitch was in a fragile state. She wasn't sure if he could handle the news that Rob had been shot. She made the executive decision to wait until tomorrow after she'd heard back from Sheila on how Rob was doing.

When she got home, she immediately set the phone tree into motion. She called Francis and Matty. They in turn called two people. In no time the whole island knew Mitch was not to hear about Rob until it was decided he could handle it. Maggie wasn't about to lose the boy to this nightmare.

Chapter Twenty-Four

Before leaving Victoria, Estelle confirmed her meetings with three film producers in Vancouver that she had in mind for a new project. Most of her clients wrote for television and film. Rob, like some of her clients, still wrote for print, but having seen the film adaptation of *One Man Against the Mountain,* he had expressed an interest in personally adapting another one of his books for film. She had been trying to convince him to start by giving nature documentaries a shot. They were no feature films when it came to pay, but they were a start.

Estelle had just left the Rosewood Hotel Georgia, in Vancouver's West End neighbourhood, when her phone rang. She didn't recognise the number. It was a 250 area code. Maybe it was business, or maybe she had left something behind in Victoria.

"Estelle Fillion speaking."

"Ms Fillion? I'm calling from the Nanaimo Regional General Hospital."

Her voice sounded young. A bit uncertain. *I am in no mood for a telemarketer at this hour.*

"Do you know a Robert Hanson?"

"Yes." Why would this telemarketer be calling about Robert? "Is there a problem?"

"Ms Fillion — I'm sorry to have to tell you this over the telephone but Mr Hanson has been in an accident. We found your name on an ICE card he was carrying in his wallet."

"Ice?"

"In case of emergency."

Estelle's knees weakened. She grabbed onto a weedy sapling planted along the sidewalk.

"Ms Fillion, are you still there?"

"Yes…you said something happened to Robert. Is he okay?"

"I'm sorry, but I am only allowed to divulge certain information over the phone. I hope you understand."

"Yes. Yes. Confidentiality. Look, I need to know if Robert is okay. If you can't tell me then…grunt or something. One for yes, two for no."

She gathered her strength. The one thing that kept racing around in her brain was *You told him to fight for this guy he'd fallen for. You made him go back.*

A bus accelerated past her filling the air with diesel fumes and noise.

"What was that? I missed that last part."

"I said he is in critical but stable condition, but — "

She cut her off. "He's still alive?"

"Yes. And he is stable."

"Thank God."

"I have to ask, are you his power of attorney?"

"I'm more than that. I'm his agent!"

* * * *

Like Estelle, Karen had decided to extend her visit to the west coast. This was her first time out here and she wasn't going to waste the opportunity. Rob couldn't object after that Oscar-winning performance she had given at Hugh McCutcheon's office.

She spent a good part of the day just wandering the streets of Victoria, avoiding, of course, the area around the politician's office. If she did run into him on the street, she doubted he would recognise her now that she had swapped out the body-hugging clothes, high-heeled shoes and makeup of Effie Perrine for the jeans, sneakers and loose sweater of an under-employed musician from Toronto.

She started with Beacon Hill Park, a picturesque seventy-three-hectare green space of trees and flowering plants. Karen spent hours meandering along the footpaths, through manicured gardens overrun with peacocks, and at the petting zoo where she found herself overwhelmed by dozens of the most adorable baby goats who divided their time equally between crawling over her and shitting — sometimes at the same time.

Next on her wish list was a must-do while in Victoria — tea at the Empress. Her guide book described it as "...a touch of England in the Canadian West. The Empress Hotel was the westernmost of the grand railway hotels scattered across the country, and afternoon tea in their elegant Lobby Lounge has been a tradition since 1908."

Karen was shown to her window seat by Monty, a very attractive twenty-something who filled out his vest and trousers quite nicely, thank you very much, and responded well to Karen's flirtations. He held out her chair for her and smiled, creating small dimples which complimented his jade-green eyes and blond-streaked hair.

"Will you be serving me?" she said in a lecherous tone that would have done Effie Perrine proud.

"I'm afraid not. That will be Christine," he replied in a heart-bursting British accent.

"What a shame," she said. "I don't think the tea will be nearly as nice."

He beamed and walked back to his station by the door. *I could eat him alive,* she thought.

Karen picked up her menu and chose the champagne tea with a glass of Veuve Clicquot Brut and smoked salmon, with a raisin scone and clotted cream. The order was taken by a very stern young woman whom she suspected might be on intimate terms with Monty and unappreciative of her earlier advances.

As she sipped her champagne, she thought, *This is the life.* Even without the champagne and over-priced tea with lox on a pancake, Victoria beat the pants off Toronto in every way — the music scene was healthier, the weather warmer, the guys cuter. It had baby goats that had climbed all over her, for crying out loud! What kept her in Toronto?

Rob, for one. He gave her security, and never asked for anything in return. He gave her a great place to stay. He covered her costs when things were tight without her even asking for help. He could just read her.

My God, she thought as she spread more clotted cream on her scone. *I take it back — these things are worth what they charge... Am I just using him? But he never complains.*

Just then her cell phone rang.

"Hello?" she answered.

"Hello. Is this Karen Salter?" asked a young female voice.

"Yes...who is this?"

"Ms. Salter, I'm calling from the Nanaimo Regional Hospital regarding Robert Hanson."

Chapter Twenty-Five

Mitch had promised Maggie before she left that he would eat and drink something, and that if he needed anything, he would call her. It had only been a week, but a diet of mushrooms and berries meant he'd lost a good deal of weight and his brain was still a little muddled. All the same, she had said that she would drop around tomorrow to check on him.

Mitch settled on a peanut butter and jam sandwich and a glass of riesling. Did they even go together? He laughed at the thought of wine pairings for childhood foods. *What would go best with s'mores?* he wondered. *A nice vidal ice wine, perhaps.*

He wolfed down the sandwich, took the wine into the living room and sat in his chair by the fire. Rufus was always torn between sitting with him or sitting by the fire. Mitch realised that if he sat here, Rufus wouldn't have had to fuss. Then something came to him. As he lay there on the Peak awaiting the rest of his life, he dreamt that Rufus had come to him. The dog had lain down beside him and rested his head on his shoulder. *I've left you a gift,* he'd said. *Whether or not you accept it is your choice.*

Now, sitting by the fire, Mitch thought about the choices he'd made throughout his life. So many were self-destructive. He had often wondered why he kept sabotaging himself. Maybe it was because he didn't deserve to be happy and when things seemed to be heading that way, he made sure it didn't happen. But now things started to come into focus. Now he had begun to remember. It was Kevin.

He remembered Sarah telling him that, as hard as it was to do, he had to stop blaming himself for things that were not in his control. He began to realise that much of what had happened to him was not his fault.

Mitch had been afraid to make the wrong decisions. He had been conditioned that way through years of "You're not going to wear that again? It makes you look fat," and "You're not going to that school, are you? I thought you were smarter than that." Mitch soon found it easier to let Kevin make the choices for him than do it himself, even though he was convinced they were the wrong ones. He had convinced himself that Kevin knew best.

Kevin had long since lost control over his own life, so he took control of his brother's.

Mitch thought about how he had chosen to believe Kevin over Rob when it came to the murder. If he'd been wrong in believing Kevin about Africa, could he also have let his brother's grudge against Rob fuel his own fears of losing him to Eric? Had Rob ever shown Mitch anything but love and support since he'd come into his life again? And the plans to develop Admiral's Peak—had Rob done anything to support it or was that idea another self-destructive move on his own part, fed by his brother?

Maybe the article Rob had written was what he claimed it to be—then Mitch remembered his laptop.

He ran into his bedroom and opened up his computer. If the file was still there, where would Rob have saved it? There, on the desktop—'Saving Marsh Island'.

He sat on the edge of his bed and read.

The article took a little more than a half an hour to read. Mitch wiped the tears from his eyes as he read the final lines over again.

"If we don't stand up for what we believe in, if we put profit ahead of what is truly precious to us, then we really are nothing more than parasites that kill their hosts."

Rob had intended to make the case to save the island from development, just as he'd said. And Mitch hadn't trusted him. Mitch had so intensely wanted to believe that he'd been betrayed because he didn't think he deserved to be happy.

* * * *

Rob lay beside him. His eyes were closed. Though he slept, his mouth held a gentle smile. He was an angel at peace with his world. Rob's muscular chest rose and fell with each breath. The sheet lay draped across his body, covering his hips. Mitch could clearly make out the outline of his cock. Mitch's heart pounded. He felt the heat of his own body as he anticipated what would come next. A small trickle of sweat traced its way from his neck, down past his nipples. His armpits dripped. Mitch's penis ached. If it was any more engorged, it would split. Precum flowed from its tip, soaking the sheet. He reached down, pulling the sheet to uncover Rob's erection –

His dream was interrupted by the ringing phone. At first, Mitch was disoriented. When he realised what it was, he wanted to ignore the phone in case it was Kevin calling. Mitch knew he wouldn't give up that easily, but if it were Maggie, and he didn't answer, she would be over here within the hour.

"Hello?"

"Hi there. Is this Mitch?" the woman said.

"Yes."

"I'm sorry to call you so early in the morning."

"No problem. It's…ten o'clock," Mitch replied.

"Ach, my internal clock is off. Travel and time zones fuck me up every time. How are you?"

"Who is this?"

"It's Karen."

"Karen?" Mitch drew a blank at the name. "I think you've got the wrong number."

"I'm Rob's friend."

"Oh…Rob's…not here."

"I know. That's what I'm trying to tell you," Karen said.

"How did you find me?" Mitch was confused.

"Rob called me a while ago, so you were in my call log. He told me to delete it but… Well, I guess it's a good thing I don't always do what he asks."

"Oh." Mitch paused. "Look, I'm not sure if Rob's told you –"

Karen pushed on. "I know how much he cares about you and I just want to make sure you're okay."

"I'm doing okay. I miss him."

"Are you going to visit him in the hospital? I'm heading up from Victoria tomorrow."

"What?" Mitch shouted. "What happened? He's in hospital?"

"Yes. That's why I called. To see if you were doing all right."

"I have no idea what's happening. I just got home from a...a trip," he said, feeling panic settling in.

"Oh shit...I thought you would have known."

"Known what?" he yelled.

"I got a call from a woman at the hospital. Then when I raised enough hell, she had a woman named Sheila call me back. Anyway, Robby was shot. Sheila said something about him going looking for you."

"Who went looking for me?"

"Robby did. He told me there'd been some sort of mix-up between you two and he wanted to set things right. He went back to the island to find you and some whack-job from the development company shot him."

Mitch was starting to comprehend. Rob's article proved it—he hadn't betrayed him. Rob must have done something to try and stop the developers... "How bad is it?"

"Sheila told me it was bad, but he's stable."

"Why didn't she tell me?" he yelled.

"I asked her. She said she didn't know where you were. Look, I don't know all of what's going on, but I know that you've got to get there. For Robby. I'm heading up as soon as my cab arrives. You'd better be there."

Karen hung up.

So, he came back for me and now he's in hospital... He picked up the phone and dialled.

"Frances? It's Mitch."

"So. You up and around?" she asked.

Mitch ignored the question. "Look, I know about Rob. I've got to get to the hospital."

"Yeah...look, I'm sorry about what happened t' your Rob," Frances said. "We were told to keep hush until you came to yer senses."

"My senses...? Never mind. It's okay. I've got to get over to the mainland as soon as possible," he continued. "Can you help?"

"Get your truck down here now and we'll get ya to where yer goin'."

"Thanks, Frances. I knew I could count on you."

He hung up, grabbed his jacket and was out the door.

As he drove to the ferry dock, he thought about what Frances had said. They were told not to tell him until he came to his senses. Until he was less fragile and could handle it, more likely. Maggie—he'd have a talk with her when he got back. And thank her. Thank all of them for protecting him. His eyes started to water. *Not now, damn it!* Maggie always said that he was the crying-est guy she'd ever met. Not that that was a bad thing. He was in touch with his emotions. *Sometimes a little too much,* he thought.

He arrived at the ferry dock. His was the only car in the loading lane. Others were pulled over at odd angles, keeping a single track open. People stood at the side of the lane, friends, mostly. One or two strangers. As Mitch drove by, he could hear people yell out, "Give Rob our best," and "Good luck." The phone tree worked quickly on the island. Up on the embankment he even saw Maggie. Their eyes met and she gave him a wave. The smile on her face said, "Love."

* * * *

Mitch boarded the vessel. In spite of the fact the boat could hold more cars, Francis closed the gate. This was to be his private ferry for the journey to Gabriola.

Frances walked up to Mitch's window as her husband piloted the boat. She smiled, saying nothing. It was a regular sailing for the first few minutes then, all of a sudden, the ferry veered to the starboard side.

Mitch was confused and thought something might be wrong.

"Is there a problem with the Gabriola dock?" Mitch asked.

"Nope," she answered.

After a few minutes Mitch asked, "Where's Francis headed?"

"Straight to Nanaimo. That's where yer headed, ain't it?"

"But are you allowed to dock there?"

"Let's see 'em stop us."

"But why?"

"This'll cut off a few hours o' travel time." She slapped her hand down on the door, fending off the impulse to wipe away a tear.

In the wheelhouse of his ferry, Francis got on the radio.

"Duke Point Terminal. Duke Point Terminal, this is the Motor Vessel *Frances 2*. Repeat, this is the Motor Vessel *Frances 2* out of Marsh Island. Over."

The radio crackled.

"Is that you, Francis?"

"It sure is. Is that Mike?"

"It sure is. Gads, it's been forever since I heard that ratty old voice o' yours." They both laughed. "What can I do fer ya?"

"Is our old pier still in one piece?"

"Sure is. They just pumped a couple o' hundred grand into fixin' it up for pleasure craft."

"Gonna need it, Mike. We got an emergency on board an' I need the okay to dock an' unload a pickup with two people bound fer the General."

"One truck, two people bound for the General. Got it, Francis. We'll clear the pier for ya. Do you need ambulance and paramedics on-site?"

"No need, Mike. Got everythin' under control. Just need the dock."

"You got it, Francis. We'll be ready for ya. Give my best to Frances for me."

"Will do, Mike. Over."

Francis leaned out the wheelhouse window and shouted, "Mike sends his regards."

"That's nice o' him to remember," Frances responded.

"Better take your position. We'll be there in a bit."

"Your position?" Mitch asked Frances.

"Yup. Yer drivin' me t' the hospital on account o' my problem."

"You've got a problem?" Mitch asked.

"Sure do, an' right about now that's gettin' you an' this truck off this ferry."

As they approached the small pier at the Duke Island Ferry Terminal, now only used to handle the large BC Ferry traffic, the islanders on the *Frances 2* could see a scurry of activity as they cleared people and equipment off the dock. The pier, according to Frances, was where their first ferry, the *Frances 1*, had docked until the ferry terminal had raised their annual fees to an astronomical level, forcing them to up and move their operation to Gabriola.

Francis manoeuvred his ship into the pier following the arm signals of a man, who Mitch found out was an old friend of Francis and Frances, Mike Williger.

As soon as the loading ramp began to lower, Frances covered herself from head to toe with a blanket and went limp in the front passenger seat of Mitch's truck, obviously exhibiting the symptoms of her problem. She looked like a large sack of potatoes.

"As soon as you get the go-ahead, drive. Don't let anybody get a good look at me," Frances whispered from beneath the blanket.

Mitch followed her instructions. As they approached the end of the pier, she told him, "Jus' drive around the corner o' that building an' let me out."

"You not coming with me?"

"No. That's a journey you have to take on your own. I have t' get back an' make Francis' supper."

Frances bailed out of the truck when they got out of sight of the terminal crew, then casually walked back. Francis kept Mike talking with his back to the pier as Frances reboarded the *Frances 2* without Mike seeing her.

"Mike, is that you?" she said joyfully. Mike spun around, surprised to see her standing there.

"Frances? Good lord, you haven't changed a bit. Still putting up with this old scow pilot?"

"Well, someone's gotta do it. He'd be lost on his own." The three had a good laugh.

"So what was the emergency all about?" Mike asked.

"Not a clue," Francis replied. "I ain't a doctor."

"An' thank God for that," Mike offered back.

They all had another good laugh.

"Well, Mike. We should give you your pier back," Francis said.

"Yup. An' we gotta get home for supper," Frances added.

"So good to see you two again. Let's not leave it so long before we do it again."

With Mike's assistance, the ferry *Frances 2* made its way out of the Duke Point control zone and back to Marsh Island with Francis and Frances holding hands in the wheelhouse.

Chapter Twenty-Six

It was a twenty-minute drive from the Duke Point Ferry Terminal to the Nanaimo Regional General Hospital. Mitch made it in ten.

He parked in the western parking lot and ran to the main patient information desk. A young man sat at the desk. He looked about eighteen, obviously a volunteer, and probably there to earn a community service credit. He was dressed in a blue and white striped shirt. His streaked, blond hair was neatly coiffed. His name badge identified him as Tylor — with an O.

Tylor heard the sound of someone running, so he looked up from his reading assignment, Jane Austin's *Pride and Prejudice*, which he found a fascinating read, though not very relevant to the life of a teenager in Nanaimo. He was startled by the fast-approaching figure. The man, unkempt and uncombed, appeared to be in distress.

Tylor's training had taught him that the best way to face a tense situation at the desk was with a wide friendly smile and a cheery welcome. Most people came into the hospital in a stressful state and just wanted to know that someone cared.

"Good morning, sir. How can I help you on this lovely day?"

"Rob Hanson...where can I find him?"

"Well, let's just see. You said his name was—or should I say *is*, if we're doing our job right." Tylor laughed at his own joke. Humour was also a way to deal with a stressful situation.

"Robert Hanson!" the man yelled, in a tone that implied he was about to tear Tylor a new asshole.

Tylor did not appreciate being yelled at. He wasn't even being paid to be here. His smile faded and he crossed his arms. That would show this man that his tone of voice was unacceptable. He didn't have to take this, even from someone who did have jet-black hair which set off his beautiful piercing blue eyes...so steamy.

"And how do you spell that?" Tylor asked curtly.

"Robert. R—O—B—"

At this point a woman who was seated in a nearby chair stood and approached.

"E—R—T. Hanson. H—A—N—S—O—N."

"Excuse me," she said. "Are you Mitch, by any chance?"

"Yeah," he replied.

"Karen. Rob's friend? I talked to you on the phone earlier."

"Oh, hi." They shook hands. "Thanks for letting me know. I'm just trying to find out from"—he looked at his badge—"Tylor here, where he is."

"Mr Hanson is currently in the ICU—"

"Great, where's that?" Mitch asked.

"You can't just go up to the ICU," Tylor said with shock.

"Why?"

"Because it's...the ICU. Not everyone can just go there. You may have germs...or something."

"Listen to me, Tylor. That man up there, he risked his life to save my home. On top of that, I haven't seen him since I thought he was a traitor and a killer from Somalia."

By this time, Tylor was questioning both his volunteer credit placement choice and his attraction to the dangerous man with the gorgeous eyes who stood breathing heavily in front of him.

"Carcross! I wondered if you'd be showing up."

Another man, with biceps thicker than Tylor's neck, strutted across the hospital lobby carrying a takeout tray of coffees. Alongside him walked an older woman in high heels, wearing a tasteful cream business suit and far too much makeup.

"You must be Mitchell," the woman said, holding out her hand. "I'm Rob's agent, Estelle. So good to finally meet you. I'm assuming you know Eric."

"Oh, we know each other," Eric said, then turned to Mitch. "I overheard your conversation with...Tylor here—is that really your name?" he asked Tylor.

"Yeah," Tylor replied, followed by an almost imperceptible giggle. If he had thought that Mitch was attractive, this tall, muscled guy was drop-dead gorgeous. "I changed the spelling so it would separate me from all the other Tylers born that year."

"And what year would that be?" Eric fished.

"Eric, you are incorrigible," Sheila said, crossing the foyer.

"Am I the only one who doesn't know what happened?" Mitch cried out.

"Probably," replied Eric. "You go wandering, you miss all the heroics."

Sheila brought things down to reality. "We'll fill you in on everything later. The most important thing is you're here. Rob's gone off for some more tests. He's doing quite well in spite of his injuries and they want to release him as soon as he has someplace safe to go."

"My place, of course," Mitch piped up. Then his face fell. "If he'll have me..."

"With what he did, I don't think there's any question as to how he feels," Estelle said.

"But the way I treated him, he must think I hate him," Mitch replied.

Estelle stared at Mitch. "Just tell him how you feel."

"Better than that," Karen interrupted. "You should do something crazy. Something huge, that'll show him how you feel."

"A grand gesture," Tylor added. The others stared at him. "Like in *Pride and Prejudice* when Mr Darcy settles all of Mr Wickham's debts and makes sure that he actually marries Lydia, making her once again respectable."

There were confused looks all around.

"Elizabeth realises there is more to Mr Darcy than meets the eye and that she does indeed love him. Good God, do none of you read?"

Karen yelled "That's it! You just have to have your...what's-his-name moment—"

"Mr Darcy," Tylor said, with a tone that revealed his disappointment in humanity.

"What he said. Find that one thing that Rob'll identify with, and you'll seal the deal."

Mitch was silent for a moment, then shouted. "I've got it! But I'll need all your help."

"Do I have to?" said Eric. "Wasn't it enough that I saved his life?"

"You saved him?" said Mitch.

"Oh, you've got to do it," Tylor begged. "You could be part of something that is so... intensely romantic."

Sheila walked up to the info desk. "Young man, you're a real literary type. Who would you say is the biggest cad in Jane Austen's novels?"

"Well, there are quite a few but, since you asked, I'd have to say...John Willoughby from *Sense and Sensibility*. Stunning good looks and a record of loving and leaving those who fall for him."

"Tylor," she said, then pointed to Eric, "meet your real-life Mr Willoughby."

* * * *

Rob was wheeled back into a new room after a series of MRIs and X-rays. He had been promoted out of ICU and into his own private room. He was exhausted. He'd climbed Everest and run out of oxygen, and felt better than this. The porter, a fit man in his late fifties, slid Rob's bed back into place and remounted his intravenous bag onto its pole.

"There you go, Mr Hanson. Get some rest now."

"Thanks, Billy."

"Hope you find this room a little less busy. Rest up good, now. They'll probably want to get rid of you as soon as they can. Hospitals are the worst place to be when you're sick." He laughed.

Billy left, and the world was quiet once again. Rob closed his eyes and drifted off to sleep.

* * * *

Mitch's house was warm with sunshine. Rob walked in from the kitchen to the living room where Mitch sat by the fire, reading. Rufus was curled up by his feet, flopped on his side with his belly towards the fire. He walked back into the bedroom where, on the dresser, lay the flower he'd presented to Mitch at dinner. He noticed that Mitch stood in the doorway.

"I wish it was real," Rob said.

"If it was real, you wouldn't have made it. This is far better."

"But it has no scent."

Mitch picked up Rob's cologne and gave the flower a light spray.

"There. Now it will always smell like you."

Mitch took him by the shoulders and swung him onto the bed. He placed his hands on Rob's stomach and slid them upwards, under his shirt and up to his shoulders. Rob lifted his arms above his head and Mitch slipped his shirt off. Mitch's hands moved back down over Rob's chest, lingering on his nipples. First his left, then his right, each caressed into hardened nubs. His lips pressed into Rob's torso, slowly working down towards his shallow navel, then following the narrow trail of fine hair towards…

* * * *

Rob woke up. Standing beside his bed was Estelle.

"What are you doing here?" he asked.

"I lied and told them I was your mother."

Rob laughed so hard his leg throbbed, but he didn't mind. Some pain was worth it.

"I hope I didn't interrupt something," she said. "You had the most delightful smile on your face while you were sleeping."

"Just a dream."

Estelle reached over and tenderly rubbed his foot.

"Look at what they've done to you, Robert. I should send you back to Africa where you'll be safer."

"I'll be fine. Just a bit of a misunderstanding."

Estelle snorted. "Misunderstandings aren't supposed to end up in criminal charges."

"You'd be surprised."

"You're probably right. So, have you had many visitors?"

"They let Sheila up for a short time when I was in ICU," he replied. "She's the vet on the island who saved my life."

"I always expected you and dogs had a lot in common. I met her downstairs. She seems like a good person. I must remember to do something nice for her."

"I think you two would get along."

"What about that man of yours? Has he been by?" she asked cautiously, trying to get a sense of how Rob was feeling about him.

"No," he said with a tone of sadness. "Strange thing was, before I was shot, I swore I saw him in the brush but apparently it was just a bear."

"Sometimes we see what we need to see."

Estelle's phone chirped with an incoming text, which she checked with no reaction.

"Always on call," Rob said with a smile. "You live for your clients. And don't think we don't appreciate it."

"Don't go making me out to be a saint. I make a bundle off some of you people. Now, enough about me. I checked with that good-looking doctor of yours and he agreed that a little stroll around the floor would do you some good."

As if on cue, Billy arrived, pushing an empty wheelchair.

"Okay, Mr H, let's get you into this thing so you can go for a ride," Billy said, carefully helping Rob out of the bed and into the chair.

"She put you up to this, didn't she?" Rob joked.

"Long ago I learned never to question a strong-minded woman," he replied with a smile. "Now, don't have him gone too long. I don't want to have to call security on you."

"What do you have against security that you would do something like that to them?" she said as she wheeled Rob out of his room.

"Lady, if you're ever looking for another man to push around, you can put my name at the top of the list!" Billy laughed.

Estelle pushed Rob to the elevator bank.

"Where are you taking me? I thought we were supposed to stick to the floor."

"You don't look all that sick. Nothing a stroll in the sunshine won't cure."

They exited the elevator at the ground floor and Estelle paused as she got her bearings.

"That's where we want to be," she said, pushing him towards the rear exit.

"I think I felt safer in Mogadishu."

Estelle pushed the automated door button and it swung open.

They exited the building into the bright sunshine of the morning. She held her course, following the sidewalk towards what looked like a green lawn, but one covered in great patches of...snow?

They turned the corner, exposing a huge expanse of white. Rob's eyes were having trouble adjusting to the brightness.

"Surprise!" yelled a familiar voice. He turned to see Karen running at him.

"What the hell are you doing here?"

"Well, what do you think?" She indicated the brilliant field of white. As his eyes adjusted, he realised that it wasn't snow. It was a field of...paper flowers, and standing in the centre was Mitch, arms outstretched. He ran to Rob, sending up a wave of paper flowers in his wake. He stopped a few yards from the wheelchair and stared at Rob.

"What did they do to you? I am so sorry."

Mitch fell on his knees. Rob wanted Mitch to hug him, to hold him tight, but instead, Mitch gently took his hand and kissed it all over.

Rob began to cry. "Oh my God, you must have been up for days making those."

"I had a lot of help. Like you did." Mitch's eyes filled with tears. "I'm sorry... I didn't have time to spray them with your favourite cologne."

"They're perfect."

Others joined the circle around Rob. He saw Sheila, and of all people, Eric.

"What are you doing here?" Rob asked.

"I stopped you from bleeding out, you ungrateful asshole," Eric said then leaned down and gave him a soft kiss on the forehead.

Rob noticed that Eric wasn't alone. Beside him stood a young guy with a blue-striped shirt. Eric had his arm around his waist.

Rob smiled. "And who might this be?"

"This is Tylor—with an O."

"Hi, Mr Hanson. I've heard a lot about you. I had to show them how to make the flowers. They'd gone through a hundred sheets of tissue paper before I rescued them." Tylor wasn't sure what to do next, so he followed Eric's lead and gave Rob an awkward kiss.

"I don't know what to say…"

"Does anybody know if Jessica is on her way?" Mitch asked the crowd.

"Who?" Rob asked.

"Your sister…" Mitch offered.

"Oh my God. I didn't think about her. She's going to kill me." Rob laughed.

"Don't worry, Robert. I'll take care of it," Estelle said. "We'll blame it on the drugs,"

"Okay, I think we'd better leave you two alone for a bit," said Karen. "Coffees in the cafeteria are on me!"

"I can get you a staff discount," Tylor piped in. "Helga in the cafeteria really likes me so I'm sure—"

"Shhhh." Eric placed his index finger on Tylor's lips and the small troupe headed off.

"I don't even know where to start explaining," said Mitch, still on his knees.

"You don't have to. If I'd been more up front with what happened in Somalia—which I've been completely cleared of, by the way—"

"And it's a good thing, too. I don't think I'm cut out to be a gangster's moll."

Rob laughed again. "I was just afraid that if you found out what happened, it would scare you away."

"I should never have listened to my brother. He just kept playing with my mind and made me doubt everything I felt."

"He always was a master at manipulating."

"Never again. I threw him out. If he even tries to come back, Frances will tear him to pieces, and that'll be a picnic compared to what I'll do to him." Anger flowed from him. Rob raised his hand to Mitch's cheek and caressed it and Mitch calmed. His muscles relaxed.

"I'll make everything as good as I can," Rob whispered.

"I know you will. But what can I do to make it up to you?"

"Well, I'm being kicked out of this place soon and I'll need a place to recover."

"I know the perfect spot. Fresh air, a full-time nurse, massages on demand."

"I can be pretty demanding."

"I just want you to know that you'll never have to worry about money. I don't have a lot, but whatever I have is yours."

"You're so sweet. Thank you." Rob paused for a moment, puzzled. "Where did that—"

Mitch interrupted "Kevin. He let me know that things were tight for writers and you could always use a little—"

"That asshole! I borrowed money from him once! That's it. One time."

"I'm sorry. Please don't be upset."

Rob started to laugh. "Money is the last thing we'll need to worry about. Writers may not make big money, but I make a living. That, plus a rather large inheritance—trust me, we'll have nothing to worry about. Just ask Karen or Estelle. They'll give me a good reference."

They both laughed.

"Throughout this whole thing," Rob said, "I've learned one thing—for the first time in my life I know that I am finally, undeniably, one hundred percent in love with someone, and that someone is right here in front of me."

Mitch began to cry. "I love you so much, and I am so sorry for everything that's —"

Rob silenced him with a gentle finger to his lips. "To quote the man I love — 'Shut up and kiss me'."

Epilogue

The sun had just risen and Mitch came into the bedroom with a fresh cup of coffee and a homemade scone with three candles burning on top.

"Ooh, thank you. Candles?" Rob asked.

"Blow them out and make a wish."

Rob laughed. Ever since he'd come home, Mitch had been celebrating one thing or another. "Okay." He closed his eyes and blew. "What's the celebration today?"

"Three months without being shot, of course."

"Of course."

"How goes the writing?"

"Not bad, seeing as how I just started. But I have it all sketched out. It won't take long to finish off the first draft." This was the first day in a long time that he had felt like himself. The new version of himself, that was. The self he always knew deep down that he wanted to be. "*One Man in Mogadishu* will be the last in the series."

"But if it's the last — won't you still be travelling?"

"I've been thinking about that. I think I travelled because I was searching for something I lost when my parents died. But I don't have to look any longer. I found that something, and it's you."

"What will you write?"

"Estelle's convinced me that I should give script-writing a shot. She thought everything we've gone through might make an interesting movie."

"Really? Who'll they get to play us?"

There was a strange sound coming from the kitchen.

"Oh. God. I forgot something. With every flaming scone you also get a gift." Mitch ran out and came back with a carton a little larger than a shoe box, which he handed to Rob. "You'd better open it quickly. I don't think it has much patience."

"What?" Rob took the box, which appeared to have a life of its own. The top sprung open and out popped a mop-haired, floppy-eared little head. "Oh my God! He's so cute? Is it a he? Where'd he come from?"

The little puppy launched itself out of the box and into Rob's arms.

"Frankly, I didn't even think to ask. It was just the cutest of the litter, and I got first pick. I didn't think I wanted another dog. I mean, no one could replace Rufus."

"Not even me?"

"Not even you. Rufus was far more obedient. But then I found out that one of Sheila's dogs was expecting, I couldn't say no, especially after she told me that the only male dog that had been near her dog when she was in heat was—"

"Rufus? This is Rufus' boy!" Rob cried, at which point he picked up the pup and looked underneath, in the back, and proclaimed, "*Girl!*" He turned the little pup around and promptly got a big lick on his nose. "Your daddy was the best dog in the world."

"She had eight healthy pups and they've all been adopted by islanders. Even Frances got one."

The three of them moved onto the bed, the puppy tumbling about between the two of them as the warm morning sun flooded the bed.

"What do you think we should call her?" Mitch asked.

"She'll let us know."

Mitch took his hand. "Come on. I have something else to show you — if you're up to it."

He took Rob out to the workshop.

"Close your eyes." He did. Mitch guided him carefully into the shop.

"Okay. Open your eyes."

What Rob saw before him took his breath away. There stood the statue of Eric as it had been the first time, but in his outstretched arms lay a new figure. The body of Rob. The fallen hero being rescued by the god.

"It was always incomplete, but I never knew what was missing. Then it came to me," he said, staring at the sculpture. "It still isn't finished. You're still a bit on the rough side."

"You're okay with me lying in his arms?" Rob asked, smiling.

"I know he's a bit of an asshole at times, but he did save you. But, if I ever find you doing this in the flesh, I'll take Sheila up on her offer to treat you like an old dog. Whatever that's supposed to mean."

"You have nothing to worry about. Nothing is worth the risk of losing you." Rob put his arms around Mitch, pulled him close, and their lips melded together, and for the first time, their souls blended into one. The woodcarver had changed his life, and Rob knew that he would never be alone again.

Testing Lysander
L.M. Somerton

Excerpt

"You need your head read, young man. You treat photography like an extreme sport."

"And your bedside manner needs some work, Doc." Brock winced and gritted his teeth as another needle punctured his flesh.

"Would you rather I patted your head and gave you a sugar lump?"

"Is that what you did in the army?" Brock often thought that his doctor forgot he was now dealing with delicate civilians.

"Most squaddies would run away screaming at the sight of a needle if it didn't mean disciplinary action. I often wish the same principles could be applied to my patients here."

Brock squirmed. "I don't remember vaccinations ever being this painful and I've had enough of them over the years"

The doctor grinned. "Baby. Okay, that was the last one. You can pull your trousers up."

He peeled off his gloves and threw the used syringe into a special bin that his nurse held out for him.

"You may experience some flu-like symptoms over the next twenty-four hours, and you'll probably get some localized bruising, but if you feel any worse than that, give me a call. When are you traveling?"

"Ten days' time." Brock smiled and got to his feet. "Then I'll be out there for four weeks. I know I should have come in sooner."

"Yes, you should. Still, better now than not at all. Well, good luck. Stay safe. Bring me back another picture for the wall in reception."

Brock pulled the consulting room door closed behind him but still overheard the doctor as he said, "Colombia! I don't know whether he's brave, stupid or just too young to know any better!"

Brock waited for the nurse to respond, but nothing happened.

"Linda! Quit mooning over him and get the room ready for the next patient."

"But he's so gorgeous, Doc. I could definitely be tempted to get unprofessional with him!"

Brock winced. *Not in this lifetime.*

The doctor chuckled. "Forget it! He's more likely to go for me than you."

There was a groan. "Oh, for goodness sake, I know it's a cliché, but I'm going to say it anyway. Why are all the pretty ones either married or gay? That is a serious loss to womankind."

Brock shook his head, stepped away from the door then headed for the exit. He didn't mind the comments. Linda said the same thing every time she saw him, and, as he used his brother's house a lot when he was traveling, that was frequently. Outside the surgery, the weather was doing its best impression of a tropical monsoon, though without the heat. The rain beat down onto pavements already awash after days of continuous downpours. In the distance, thunder rumbled ominously and the sky had a threatening purple hue that spoke of more rain to come.

Brock looked up just as lightning split the sky. The rain got even harder. He turned up the collar of his waterproof coat and grimaced at the trickle of cold water that immediately slid down his neck. In seconds, his hair was soaked and plastered to his head. He hunched his shoulders and lengthened his stride toward home — though it wasn't strictly his home. He was just house-sitting while his brother, sister-in-law and two young nephews spent their annual fortnight's holiday on one of the Balearic Islands — he couldn't remember which one.

Brock spent such a lot of time traveling on photographic assignments that he'd never bothered to get his own place. When he was in England, he spent the time with his brother's family or returned to his mum and dad's rambling old place in Northumberland. Their house was so big, and they were both so busy with various pet projects and charities, that he could probably have lived there full-time without them even noticing his presence. Brock smiled to himself at the thought — he was very fond of his eccentric parents.

He soon arrived at the edge of the new estate where his brother's house sat on a decent-sized plot, halfway down a tree-lined avenue. Despite the miserable weather, he felt uncomfortably warm and was glad to make it to the sanctuary of the front hall, where a small puddle gathered around his feet as he stripped off dripping outdoor clothes and boots. Feeling progressively worse, he caught his reflection in the hall mirror and grimaced. His skin appeared clammy and his hands shook a little.

"Bloody vaccinations," he muttered. He climbed the stairs slowly, passing a number of his own framed photographs, and headed for the guest room bed. "Better just sleep it off." He grabbed a towel from the en suite, gave his hair a rub then stripped to his underwear. Drawing the curtains, he frowned at the sheets of driving rain. He could just make out the shape of a man sheltering under a tree opposite the house. "Blimey, he must be soaked." Despite his desire to get into his comfy bed to sleep away the after-effects of his inoculations as quickly as possible, Brock shrugged into his dressing gown then went back downstairs to the hallway to grab an umbrella. If the guy had to be outside, at least he could stay a little drier. By the time he went to the front door, the man was gone. Had he even been there, or was it a side-effect of the injections the doctor hadn't warned him about? He trudged back to the bedroom, finished pulling the curtains closed then took off his robe. He slid gratefully between cool sheets as his body reacted to the cocktail of drugs swimming through his system. Sleep came quickly and he drifted into dreams of distant jungles and the amazing pictures he would take.

* * * *

Outside, under the dripping tree, Kyle Dawson shifted uncomfortably. He had just been treated to a glimpse of the most tempting body he'd seen in some time and his cock had started dancing to its own tune despite the cold, damp conditions. He shook water droplets from the caped shoulders of his long, waxed coat and tilted the brim of his hat forward a bit further. Kyle knew exactly where the subject of his observation had been that day, indeed for the last two weeks, though today was the first time he had gotten close to Brock's home.

He closed his eyes and recalled the details of the file he had been given. *Lysander Brock, known as Brock to his friends* — parents clearly had a thing for Shakespeare because his brother's name was Ferdinand. *Six feet tall, blond hair, blue eyes* — stunning blue eyes in Kyle's opinion — *one-hundred-eighty pounds* — all completely edible — *aged twenty-five. Permanent address listed at his parents' home in Northumberland. Professional photographer with work published in every travel and wildlife publication worth reading. Very well-traveled, with skills that included caving, climbing and hiking. Currently unattached. Two previous boyfriends known, neither particularly serious.*

Or deserving, Kyle thought grumpily.

He pictured the photo hidden in his inside pocket and licked his lips. He knew he should be maintaining a cold, clinical approach to the task ahead but, for Christ's sake, this guy was stunning and there was no harm in dreaming. After all, he'd been chosen for the job specifically because he was also gay. His bosses had thought he would blend in better if he needed to follow his quarry to gay pubs and clubs, though, in the end, that had not been necessary. Lysander Brock led a very quiet life when he wasn't working.

"You'd have no chance, you idiot," Kyle muttered under his breath, "even if you weren't about to ruin his day."

He looked around to make sure he was unobserved then crossed the road. The appalling weather worked in his favor, as very few people were out and about. Confident that there was no one around to witness his swift journey across the garden and, through the unlocked gate, he slipped down the path at the side of the house and into the back garden of the property. Tall hedges and mature trees shielded it from the neighboring houses, giving him all the time in the world to pick the lock on the door and slip into the kitchen.

Kyle found the back door key on a wall hook. He relocked the door, slid the additional bolt shut and tucked the key into his pocket. Taking his time, he removed his wet coat and hat and hung them over a chair. The layout of the house was stored in his head so he moved confidently to the front door to set the deadbolts. Secure in the knowledge that Brock would not be able to run, he crept up the stairs and peered around the door of the guest bedroom. Kyle had to bite down on his lip as he saw the young man in the bed, sound asleep. Brock had pushed the covers down to his hips, one arm was flung out to the side and his smooth, hairless chest rose and fell gently as he breathed. His face was a little flushed but, other than that, he seemed at peace. Kyle resisted the temptation to pull the covers down a little farther, backed away then crept downstairs to the kitchen. He took one of the chairs set around the kitchen table and turned it so that he could face the door to the hall then he settled down to wait.

About the Author

Peter E. Fenton's previous work was focused on writing for the stage, with award-winning productions of *The Giant's Garden, Newfoundland Mary*, and *Bemused.*

He spent many years working in palaeontology in remote locations including the Canadian Rockies, the Northwest Territories and Nunavut.

Peter lives in Toronto, Canada with his partner of more than twenty years, Scott White. At heart, he is an incredible romantic.

The Woodcarver's Model is his first novel.

Peter loves to hear from readers. You can find his contact information, website details and author profile page at https://www.pride-publishing.com

PUBLISHING

Sign up for our newsletter and find out about all our romance book releases, eBook sales and promotions, sneak peeks and FREE romance books!